Hunted in the
ALASKAN WILDERNESS
LEE RODDY

PUBLISHING

Colorado Springs, Colorado

HUNTED IN THE ALASKAN WILDERNESS
Copyright ©1996 by Lee Roddy

Library of Congress Cataloging-in-Publication Data

Roddy, Lee, 1921–
    Hunted in the Alaskan Wilderness / Lee Roddy.
       p. cm.—(A Ladd Family Adventure ; 13)
    Summary: When Josh and his family move to Alaska, the twelve-year-old
explores his new neighborhood, gets caught up in wilderness adventures, and
learns lessons of friendship and trust.
    ISBN 1-56179-445-7
    [1. Alaska—Fiction. 2. Wilderness areas—Fiction. 3. Adventure and adven-
tures—Fiction.] I. Title. II. Series: Roddy, Lee, 1921– Ladd family adventure ; 13.
PZ7.R6Hu   1996
[Fic]—dc20   95-47224
                                                       CIP
                                                       AC

Published by Focus on the Family Publishing,
Colorado Springs, Colorado 80995.
Distributed in the U.S.A. and Canada by Word Books, Dallas, Texas.

The author is represented by the literary agency of Alive Communications,
1465 Kelly Johnson Blvd., Suite 320, Colorado Springs, CO 80920.

This is a work of fiction, and any resemblance between the characters in this book
and real persons is coincidental.

Focus on the Family books are available at special quantity discounts when purchased
in bulk by corporations, organizations, churches, or groups. Special imprints, messages,
or excerpts can be produced to meet your needs. For more information, write: Special
Sales Department, Focus on the Family Publishing, 8605 Explorer Dr., Colorado Springs,
CO 80920; or call (719) 531-3400 and ask for the Special Sales Department.

Cover Illustration: Paul Casale
Cover Design: James Lebbad

Printed in the United States of America

96 97 98 99 00/10 9 8 7 6 5 4 3 2

To my second-born grandson, SCOTT
~~Zachary de Haas,~~
a special boy who brightens our lives

from·

GRANDPA
&

GRAM MA H.

·1997

CONTENTS

ACKNOWLEDGMENTS

The author wishes to express his deep appreciation for interviews with dozens of people in Alaska and especially those who contributed to the factual research in this book, including:

Paul Jobe, founder-owner of Wild Alaska Rivers Company, Anchorage.

Steve Ortland, artist and former fishing guide, and his wife, Romney, of Anchorage.

Lt. Col. Mark Barnett, physician, U.S. Air Force, and his wife, Karen, and their sons of Eagle River, now moved to Ohio.

Brian Trimble, M.D., neurologist at the Alaskan Native Hospital in Anchorage and a board member of the Alaska Private and Home Educators' Association (APHEA), and his wife, Mary, and family of Eagle River.

Matthew and Susan Teel and family of Chugiak.

Home-school students at Grace Brethren Church in Eagle River.

Chapter One

A WILD BEAR ON DECK

In sudden disappointment, Josh Ladd gripped the phone tighter and protested, "But, Dad, you promised!"

"Hold on, son!" his father interrupted gently. "I said I would *try* to take you tonight. But moving and starting the paper has been much more time-consuming than I expected."

Josh didn't reply. He knew his dad was right—moving to Alaska from Hawaii and launching a newspaper for tourists had been demanding. Josh jumped up from the living room floor, where he had been sitting surrounded by huge cardboard boxes waiting to be unpacked.

"Son, you still there?" Mr. Ladd asked.

"Yes, Dad," Josh said. He heard his mother and older sister in the kitchen unwrapping dishes that had been packed in old newspapers.

"Please try to understand, son."

"I'm trying," Josh answered, but that was difficult since he hadn't seen much of his dad lately. Josh had looked forward to attending the father-son dinner at church that evening. He was disappointed that his dad

1

wouldn't make it.

Mr. Ladd had come to Alaska a month ahead of his wife and children. Yesterday morning, the rest of the family arrived at the house he had rented outside of Anchorage*.The moving van had showed up at midday, and everyone except his father had been trying to get settled. Mr. Ladd spent 16 hours daily in his downtown office 12 miles from home.

His voice came over the wire. "You still there?"

"Yes, Dad." Josh paused, then asked, "What about our fishing trip with Tank and his father? Are we going to have to miss that, too?"

"I hope not. I want us to have that first wilderness experience together. Since I've been working late so many nights, I think I might get things under control in a few days."

"I understand," Josh replied dully.

After hanging up, the 12-year-old boy called, "Mom, Dad's going to be late again tonight."

"I'm not surprised," she replied from the kitchen. "But that's okay. I'll take you and Tank to your meeting."

"It's for fathers and sons," Josh reminded her. "I can probably go with Tank and his dad, but it won't be the same."

Coming to stand in the doorway while unwrapping a plate, Mrs. Ladd said, "Your father is doing the best he can."

---

*The definition and pronunciation of words marked by asterisks are contained in a glossary at the end of the book.

"Tank's father just moved here, too, but *he's* been getting home for dinner."

"Sam Catlett is the manager of a department store, which is a heavy responsibility. Your father is co-owner of a newspaper. That's a different kind of responsibility. Your father could lose every penny we have if the publication fails."

Josh was going to respond when the phone rang. "I'll get it," he said and lifted the receiver. Before he could even say hello, he heard Tank's excited voice.

"There's a bear at our house!"

"A what?"

"A bear!" Tank Catlett's usually slow, easygoing manner of speaking speeded up with excitement. "It's climbing up our back lanai*!"

"Oh, sure—a bear," Josh scoffed. "And you mean your deck or porch. In Hawaii, it was called a lanai, but not here."

"Whatever you call it," Tank interrupted, "a bear is climbing it!"

Josh chuckled. "Right! We're just outside the largest city in Alaska and—"

"I'm not kidding!" Tank's words were coming in a high, excited rush. "A big, old black bear is climbing up that 12-foot post that supports the right side of our back deck!"

Josh tensed. "You're serious?"

"Of course! And I'm home alone. What should I do?"

"Stay calm! I'll be right there!"

"Okay, but be careful," Tank said. "Make sure the bear isn't in front of the house when you come."

"Right!" Josh slammed down the phone. "Mom!" he called, dodging boxes in a mad rush for the front door. "I'm going to Tank's house!"

"Hey, wait a minute," his 14-year-old sister, Tiffany, said from the kitchen. "You're just trying to get out of unpacking!"

"No I'm not. This is important!" Josh assured her, grabbing the doorknob.

"What's going on?" his mother asked.

"Tell you later!"

Josh didn't hear his mother's reply as he darted out the door, through the wire gate in the four-foot-high fence, and down the short gravel driveway. He turned left onto Sourdough* Street, racing from his corner house.

A bear! Josh exclaimed to himself as he ran, his tennis shoes crunching on the graveled street. *It must have come out of the forest behind Tank's house!*

Josh raced past six houses, three on each side of the street, all with large yards. The homes were widely separated and tucked back from a giant shelf of land that had been carved out of the mountains with as little disturbance to the environment as possible.

The upscale Alaskan neighborhood of Fireweed* was nestled between two major river valleys and between the communities of Eagle River and Chugiak*. All are in south-central Alaska and within the municipality of Anchorage.

Fireweed was not at all like Honolulu*, Josh had decided. There, houses and apartments were close together.

All were connected by paved streets. Here, the three communities were surrounded by a wilderness of forested mountains rising 2,000 feet.

Fireweed, named after an Alaskan flower, more closely resembled a wilderness, except for the areas where human beings had carefully made places to live. The graveled roads threaded down from the modern residential district through the mountains to paved Skyline Loop. This street connected Fireweed residents to the modern, six-lane Glenn Highway leading to downtown Anchorage. A quarter of a million people lived there—or about half the people in the forty-ninth state.

Panting a little from his hard run, Josh passed the last house on Sourdough. Through a break in the mountain ranges, Josh glimpsed Anchorage, which was spread out on a plain. The city ended at the shimmering bodies of water known as Cook Inlet* and Knik Arm*.

Josh turned right onto an unpaved, dead-end street named Clouds Rest. It led up a slight incline with one small, yellow house almost hidden by trees on the left. Beyond that, Tank and his family had moved into the spacious home snuggled up against the forested hillside.

Puffing up the hill, Josh slowed down and looked around cautiously to make sure the bear hadn't come around to the front of the house. Suddenly, he was startled to hear a man's angry shout from inside the yellow house.

"Alex, you dumb kid! Can't you ever do anything right?"

A boy answered, "I'm sorry, Uncle Bill!"

"Being sorry won't help, Alex! Stop doing stupid things!"

Josh cringed but kept running. He had never been yelled at like that, and he felt bad for the boy.

Tank met Josh at the front door of his new home. "Hurry up!" he urged, motioning for Josh to follow.

"I'm hurrying!" Josh forgot about his father's disappointing phone call and the disturbing voices he had just overheard. "Where are your mother and sister?"

"They went to town," Tank replied, leading the way past a small bench where muddy shoes or boots were usually removed in winter before entering the main part of the house. The boys threaded their way past living room furniture and partially opened boxes spread haphazardly around the floor.

Both boys were big for their age. Tank was only two months older than Josh but outweighed him by 10 pounds. Tank's straight blond hair was still bleached almost white from the Hawaiian sun, and his nose still showed the signs of perpetual peeling. Josh had wavy brown hair and intense blue eyes. Except for their size and broad shoulders, Josh was the opposite of Tank. He tended to move and talk fast while Tank usually did everything slowly.

"That bear has about torn up the barbecue," Tank explained, as he led Josh through the living room and into the kitchen, heading toward the back door. "My dad fixed fresh salmon last night, and I forgot to clean the grill. The bear must have smelled the salmon. I hope Dad doesn't ground me for that!"

Easing up to the large sliding door that opened onto the spacious deck, both boys peered through the glass. The barbecue had been knocked over and the utensils scattered.

"He's gone!" Tank said disappointedly.

"He couldn't have gone far." Josh cautiously slid open the door, double-checked the deck, then ran to the back railing. "Maybe we can still see him."

The boys looked over the railing hopefully. The only things in sight were the cottonwood, aspen, and spruce trees growing nearby and the mountainside, which rose steeply only 50 feet from the house.

Josh glanced at the densely forested mountainside and sighed. "I sure wish I could have seen him. It would've been great to write all our friends in Honolulu about that."

"Yeah," Tank agreed glumly.

"You could write them," Josh said. "Roger and Manuel would get a big kick out of hearing from you."

"You know I hate to write letters," Tank said, leading the way back into the house. "You want something to drink?"

"No, thanks. I've got to get back home and help unpack. Mom will probably be calling here to see why I left so fast after you called."

"When are we going to explore these mountains?" Tank asked, motioning toward the range behind the house.

"Soon as we can." Josh stopped at the front door. "It would be best to go with some guys who know the area so we don't get lost."

Josh wanted to mention that his father would not be able to go with Tank and his dad to the meeting that night, but Tank spoke first.

"I saw a couple of boys watching us when we moved in. Maybe we could ask them to show us around."

Josh frowned. "That reminds me. I feel sorry for the kid who lives in that yellow house in front of yours." He told Tank about hearing a man's angry shouts and a boy's timid reply. "I'll bet he could use a friend," Josh added.

Always cautious, Tank shook his head dubiously. "I don't know about that. Whoever shouted at him could be mean to us, too."

"Maybe so, but that's all the more reason that boy needs a friend." He reached for the front door. "Well, I'd better get home."

Walking toward his house, Josh was alert to the possibility that the bear might emerge on the road in front of him. When he heard a faint sound off to his right, Josh stopped suddenly. He listened for a moment, ready to run back to Tank's house if a bear appeared.

Wait a minute. That sounds like somebody crying, Josh decided. He eased toward the sound, quietly pushing through heavy brush.

From the trees ahead of him, Josh heard angry words. "I can't do anything right!"

Josh stopped, startled by the hostile tone.

"Uncle Bill doesn't want me, and I don't want to be here. I should run away, but I can't even do that right. What if Louie finds us? I can't take this anymore!" The boy's voice rose in a plaintive wail, followed by a sob.

Instantly concerned, Josh started forward again and stopped abruptly when a red-haired boy of about 11 whirled around. The boy's green eyes opened with surprise, and he leaped from a stump where he had been sitting. His mouth opened, but he didn't say anything.

Josh tried to smile. "Hi." He hesitated, but when the boy didn't answer, Josh continued. "You okay?"

The smaller boy brushed tears from his heavily freckled face, but still he didn't answer.

Josh tried again. "I'm Josh Ladd. My family and I just moved into that white house down the street. My best friend, Tank Catlett, lives—"

"Leave me alone!" the boy blurted.

Josh blinked but stood still. "Is there anything I can do?"

"No!" The boy shook his head violently. "Nobody can help. Nobody!" He turned and plunged into the trees.

Josh watched in bewilderment as the boy disappeared. *I wonder what that was about?* Josh thought. After a moment's reflection, he turned back toward Tank's home. When he arrived, Josh quickly told his friend what had happened, then added, "I'm sure that's the same kid I heard being yelled at earlier. I think the man called him Alex."

Sighing and shaking his head, Tank said, "I expected it would be nice and peaceful here in the mountains and trees."

"What do you think he meant by saying his uncle doesn't want him? Where do you suppose his parents are?"

"Who knows?" Tank said.

"Let's go see if we can find him."

Tank was reluctant, but as always, he followed Josh. They started down the hill, hoping to catch a glimpse of the red-haired boy. But there was no sign of him and no sound from the small house hidden in the trees.

"Well," Josh said with a disappointed sigh when they had passed the house, "I guess he's still out in the woods somewhere."

"That could be dangerous," Tank said. "We know bears live there, and my dad warned Marsha and me to be careful of moose. In fact, there was a story on the radio this morning about a man being killed by a moose near Anchorage."

"Really?"

"I heard it myself," Tank solemnly declared. "It's sure different from Honolulu," he added. "No wonder they say Alaska is the last frontier. It's sort of like the rest of the country a hundred years ago."

"It really is," Josh agreed, turning to look through a break in the Chugiak Range to the city spread out on the plain beyond. "But in some ways, Alaska is very modern."

"My dad says that's mostly true of Anchorage. In fact, he said there's a saying, 'Anchorage is only a half hour from Alaska.'"

A distant flash of silver showed where a commercial jetliner slanted across Knik Arm to land at Anchorage International Airport.

Tank said, "That water looks a little like the Pacific Ocean off Honolulu, doesn't it?"

"Sort of." Turning back to look up the gravel road, Josh said, "I wonder if we should knock on the door and tell that man that the redheaded kid might be in danger out in the woods."

"They've lived here longer than we have, so they must know about the dangers. Besides, I don't think we should mess with things that don't concern us."

"How would you feel if something bad happened to him and we hadn't tried to help?"

Tank protested, "You sure know how to hit where it hurts."

Josh grinned and playfully poked his friend in the ribs. "Doesn't what I said make sense?"

Tank tried to keep from returning the grin. "If I listen to you one more second, you're going to get us into trouble again!"

"We've always survived, haven't we? Let's do it."

Without waiting for an answer, Josh started to walk toward the small house.

With a groan, Tank followed.

Chapter Two

THE MYSTERIOUS STRANGER

Inside the house, the red-haired boy carefully peered through the tan blinds. "Two kids are coming to the door," he announced without looking around.

"Get away from there!" The man's sharp tone cut through the tiny room. It was sparsely furnished with an old sofa, a tattered recliner, a mismatched ottoman, and a scarred coffee table. There were no pictures on the walls. Everything suggested this was a temporary residence for the two occupants.

The boy quickly stepped back from the blinds and turned around. He had to open his mouth twice before he got enough courage to speak.

"Uncle Bill," he asked plaintively, "aren't you ever going to let me have any friends?"

"No, Alex. Not until I think it's safe." He was a skinny man of about 40, medium height, with hazel eyes, dyed black hair, and a two-day growth of pale-blond whiskers on a long, slender face.

Alex wanted to cry out, "That's what you said in

Indiana and California! Then you said it would be safe up here because Louie couldn't find us!" But he knew better than to protest, so he kept quiet.

His uncle pulled out a pack of cigarettes and shook one out while glowering at his nephew. "I wouldn't have this problem if it wasn't for you and—" He broke off abruptly at the sound of a knock on the door.

They both turned to look at the door. It was solid wood to withstand Alaska's winters.

"I'll get it," Bill announced. "You keep quiet."

As Alex flopped dejectedly onto the couch, his uncle opened the door a crack and peered out. "Yeah?"

Alex heard a boy's voice.

"I'm Josh Ladd and this is Tank Catlett. We're your new neighbors. We just moved into the neighborhood and saw your nephew. We wonder if he—"

"Nephew?" the man interrupted sharply. "You saw my son. What makes you think he's my nephew?"

Josh drew back slightly. He hesitated, unwilling to say he had seen the boy crying and heard him talking to himself. "Uh," Josh stammered, "I thought ... "

"Well, don't! Anyway, he's busy." The door closed with finality, and the man whirled to face the redheaded boy.

"How did he know you're my nephew?"

"I ... I ... "

"I told you not to talk to anybody. Now, when did you talk to that kid?"

Alex hadn't looked closely at the boy who had found him talking to himself. When he glanced out the window a few moments ago, he had noticed that one boy was blond. Alex thought the dark-haired boy might be the one who had surprised him earlier, but he wasn't sure, and he certainly wasn't going to confess that encounter to his uncle.

"I . . . I didn't really talk to him, Uncle Bill."

"Don't lie to me, Alex!"

The boy cringed but shook his head vigorously. "I'm not! I ran into the woods when I saw him."

The man scowled. "Well, I don't like it. If I ever see you talking to any of those kids . . . "

"I won't, honest!"

His uncle regarded him with suspicious eyes. Alex turned away and leaned across the back of the sofa. He pulled the blinds back just enough to peer around them. The two boys stood uncertainly on the porch, looking at each other.

"They gone?" Uncle Bill asked.

"They're turning to go." Alex watched them leave the front stoop and head toward the graveled street.

"Then get away from the window, Alex. You'll make them suspicious if they see you peeking out at them."

Alex wanted to say, "What do you think you just did? If anyone made them suspicious, it was you." But he kept quiet. Nothing he said made any difference anyway.

In the past few months since Alex had come to stay with his only living relative, Alex had thought of running away. But he wasn't old enough to take care of himself, and he was afraid to even try. He thought longingly about how much he would enjoy knowing those boys. But they had been sent away, just as others had wherever Alex and his uncle had briefly lived.

Uncle Bill commented softly, "Louie's real good at finding people. We've been lucky to be tipped off each time he closed in on us."

Not us—you, Alex thought. *He's not after me. I didn't do anything.* Then he silently added, *But that might not stop Louie from hurting me, too.*

* * *

Walking toward the street, Tank mused, "Not very friendly, was he, Josh?"

"No, he sure wasn't." Josh frowned thoughtfully, remembering the kid he had seen crying by the roadside. "I tried to look past that man to see that red-haired boy, but I didn't see him."

The two friends reached the street just as a wolflike dog ran barking from the dense undergrowth. Josh and Tank spun to face the 100-pound animal.

At the same moment, a couple of boys about their age emerged from the brush. The taller boy shouted, "Willi, no!" As the dog slowed, the boy called to Josh and Tank, "He won't hurt you."

"I'm glad for that," Tank murmured.

Josh noticed that the dog had a distinctive dark cap and white mask with dark eyes. Its bushy tail, curling inward over the back, began to wag. Josh let the dog sniff his hand before asking, "What's his name?"

"Williwaw*, or Willi for short," the owner replied as the boys met in the center of the lightly traveled road. "He's a malamute* mix. Williwaw is actually the name for a strong Alaskan wind. Willi runs around like that—real fast and powerful. That's how he got his name."

The shorter boy gave his friend a nasty look. "I'd rather have a husky. They're smaller, but they sometimes have light eyes. I like that."

Josh commented, "Willi sort of looks like a wolf."

"If you see him running loose at night, you'll think he's a wolf," his owner declared proudly. "But Willi's fine, unless kids get to scuffling. Then sometimes he nips them. I guess he thinks they're fighting, and he doesn't like that."

The shorter boy announced with a hint of self-importance, "I'm Ryan Spitzer, and this is Jacob Ashton. We live there." He pointed to houses facing each other on opposite sides of the street.

"Hi," Jacob said quietly. He was half a head taller than Ryan. Josh and Tank were a couple inches taller than Jacob.

Josh and Tank introduced themselves and said they had just moved to the area. They pointed toward their homes.

"We know," Ryan said, thrusting his chin out pugnaciously. "Me and Jacob watched you both move in. Where you guys from?"

"Hawaii," they answered together.

Ryan made a face. "That place is nothing compared to Alaska. This is the greatest state of them all."

"We've lived in California and Hawaii, and we liked both places," Tank said. "We expect to like Alaska, too."

Ryan asked, "You guys got any brothers or sisters?"

"An older sister and a younger brother," Josh said.

"I've got a sister named Marsha," Tank added. "Both she and Josh's sister are the same age."

"Sisters!" Ryan rolled his eyes. "I got three, and each is more of a pain than the other. No brothers."

"Tiffany's 14," Josh explained. "She's okay most of the time, except when she gets bossy."

Jacob said, "I'm the only one besides my parents."

Josh turned to face the small house. "Do you two know the redheaded kid who lives up there?"

"No, he keeps to himself," Ryan explained. "He and his dad just moved in a couple days before you two did."

"His dad?" Josh asked. "You met him?"

"No," Ryan admitted, "but I've seen him."

Josh said, "I thought I heard him call the man Uncle Bill."

Ryan shrugged. "Uncle, Dad, who cares? They're about as friendly as two wolverines*."

Jacob volunteered, "I think they recently arrived from Outside."

"Outside?" Tank asked.

Ryan shook his head sadly, as though Tank wasn't too bright. "We say Outside when we mean any place outside of Alaska. I think they came from the Lower Forty-Eight*."

Tank looked puzzled, so Josh quickly explained, "I think that's like the expression we used in Hawaii—there we called the rest of the nation the Mainland."

Tank scowled. "Sounds to me as if you guys in Alaska forgot about Hawaii. It's a state, too, you know, but you only mentioned 48."

Ryan snapped, "Alaska's better than all the others."

Josh, sensing Ryan's feistiness, grinned and exchanged a quick glance with Tank. "I'll remember that."

"I can beat up on any kid in this whole neighborhood," Ryan unexpectedly announced, puffing up his chest and shooting a challenging look at Josh and Tank.

Josh tried to keep a straight face. "You won't have any trouble with Tank or me."

Ryan looked relieved. "Just don't forget it," he warned.

Josh glanced at Jacob, who seemed embarrassed by his friend's belligerence.

Jacob pointed toward the house where the mysterious man and boy lived. "A few days ago, my dog ran into his yard, and that man opened the door and yelled at me. I haven't seen the boy outside since they moved in."

Josh decided not to say anything about finding him crying or hearing the man yell at the boy. Instead, he asked, "How safe is it to go exploring in the mountains around here?"

"They're called the Chugiak Range, and they're safe enough," Ryan said, "but you still have to watch out for wild animals and things like devils club."

"What's that?" Josh asked.

"It's a vicious plant with huge leaves that fill you full of splinters if you touch it," Ryan explained. "Sort of like porcupine quills that feel like bee stings."

Jacob said, "It's much worse than stinging nettle."

Ryan scowled as if he didn't want Jacob's help in telling about the plant. "The devils club stalk is even worse than the leaves," Ryan continued. "Some stickers on the leaves are so small they're almost like hairs. First, you get little red bumps, and then you can get an infection. It'll keep stinging until you get all the stickers out. Even so, it still hurts for a day or two."

"It's really bad stuff," Jacob agreed. "So if you run into it, you'd better hope someone has a pair of tweezers and some lotion, like the kind used for treating poison oak."

"Of course," Ryan added, "in the woods you might see several kinds of animals—coyotes, lynx, porcupines, plus moose and bears."

Tank declared, "I saw a bear on our back deck a while ago, in broad daylight."

Ryan scoffed. "Everyone in Fireweed has seen a bear, moose, or some other wild animal in their yard or garage."

"That's right," Jacob agreed. "Especially in the winter, you'll have—"

"Black bears, mostly," Ryan interrupted. "Most of the time, they won't bother you. But you can't tell about grizzlies. Sometimes they'll run from you, but other times they'll charge."

Jacob declared, "My dad has a couple of books with hundreds of true stories about bear attacks."

"I've read those books," Ryan declared. "Some black bears will attack, but it's usually coastal browns* and some inland grizzlies. In fact, two people recently got mauled by a grizzly just outside of Anchorage. And there was a story in the paper about some fishermen—"

"Fishermen! That reminds me," Josh interrupted, ignoring Ryan's frown. "Tank, I forgot to tell you. My dad says he can't take me to the meeting tonight, but he still hopes to make our fishing trip."

"You can ride with us tonight," Tank replied. "But it'd be a real bummer not to go on the fishing trip."

Josh answered solemnly, "It sure would. Our first in Alaska. Well, I'd better get home and finish unpacking the things for my room."

"I'll help you," Tank volunteered. "When my mom and sister get back, I'll go home and finish our unpacking."

"Are you afraid of being home alone in case that bear comes back?" Ryan asked with a hint of sarcasm.

Josh sensed his best friend starting to bristle, so he said jokingly, "Maybe Tank's afraid he'd scare the bear."

Tank relaxed. "That's right. Come on, Josh. Let's go."

The friends walked toward Josh's home, leaving the other two boys behind.

Josh felt a tinge of annoyance at Ryan. He seemed to have an opinion about everything and had no hesitancy in expressing it. He also seemed to dominate Jacob, who appeared to be a nice person.

Tank muttered under his breath, "In Hawaii, we had big, old, mean King Kong. Here, we've got a little banty rooster* with a big mouth and a monstrous ego."

"Let's just hope we can keep on his good side."

"Why?" Tank demanded. "He wouldn't have a chance

against either of us."

"I know, but let's avoid trouble if we can." Josh turned and looked back at the house where the red-haired boy lived. "I wonder what's going on there?"

* * *

Alex watched Josh and Tank through the blinds and then announced quietly, "They're gone."

"Good!" Uncle Bill vigorously snuffed his cigarette into a coffee-can lid sitting on the scarred coffee table in front of him. "I'm going to dye your hair later today."

"I told you why I don't want to, Uncle Bill," Alex weakly protested. "My red hair is all I've got left that feels like me. I don't even have my own name anymore."

Nervously lighting another cigarette, the man blew smoke toward the boy before answering. "I'm sure that's how Louie found us before. Now listen, I'm going to change and drive into Anchorage. You lay low, you hear me?"

"Yes." Alex turned away from the smoke and coughed. He stifled his hurt feelings and abruptly headed down the hall to his bedroom.

This is so unfair! he told himself fiercely, entering his sparsely furnished room. He threw himself across the unmade bed. *I've got to get out of this somehow. I've got to! But how?*

* * *

Josh had almost finished telling Tank about his father's phone call when the two friends neared the Ladds' house.

They spotted Josh's 10-year-old brother, Nathan, who was walking up Skookum* Drive at the intersection of Sourdough Street. Nathan waved at them.

"Let's wait here for him," Tank suggested.

Josh nodded, watching his little brother saunter toward them. Just then, a big, black luxury car came alongside Nathan and stopped.

Josh watched the driver's side window roll down. A man with a black hat stuck his head out and called to the younger boy.

Josh frowned. "Nathan's not supposed to talk to strangers."

"The guy's probably just asking directions. Anyway, Nathan's staying out of the guy's reach."

"Just the same," Josh said, "let's get down there."

They hurried toward Nathan as the car's electric window slid up so Josh couldn't see the driver's face. The car moved up the hill past the boys and vanished around a curve at the base of the mountain.

"What did that man want, Nathan?" Josh asked.

"He was looking for somebody," Nathan explained. He was short for his age, but in every other way, he was a typical 10-year-old.

"Who?" Josh asked.

The younger boy picked up a pebble from the road and threw it at a tree. "Some redheaded kid."

Josh and Tank stopped abruptly and looked down at Nathan with sudden interest.

Josh asked, "What did you tell him?"

"I told him that we just moved in, and I hadn't seen any redheaded guy. But my new friend had told me that several kids lived up the hill on Skookum, just around the curve. So I told the man that."

Tank looked at Josh. "Are you thinking what I am?"

"I sure would like to know what's going on."

"Yeah!" Tank agreed. "So would I."

"Great!" Josh exclaimed. "Let's find out!"

Chapter Three

ALEX'S LONELY FEARS

From his bedroom, Alex heard his uncle's car start and back out of the garage. *He won't let me have any friends*, he thought, *but what's he going to do when school starts? I'll make friends there.*

Moments later, Alex was startled when he heard the front door hurriedly unlock. He jumped up and ran down the hallway just as his uncle stepped inside wearing dark glasses and a brown hat pulled low on his forehead.

"He's here!" Uncle Bill exclaimed. He shut the door and moved to the window to peer through the blinds.

"Who's here?" Alex asked.

"Louie! Who else?" Uncle Bill backed away from the window and reached for his cigarettes, his hand shaking. "He's closing in on us again!"

"Are you sure?"

"Certainly! I saw him drive up in one of those big, fancy cars he likes to rent. He stopped a little kid. I'm sure he asked if the kid had seen you and that blasted red hair."

Alex's anxiety increased along with his uncle's, but he

managed to say hopefully, "Maybe it wasn't him. Did you get a good look?"

"I didn't have to, Alex. I'm positive that's who it was. Now shut up and let me think."

Alex sank into the sofa in despair, unconsciously wrapping his arms around himself. *It's the same old story all over again*, he told himself.

It had been that way for the past three months since Alex had been forced to live with his uncle. Run. Hide. Try to breathe freely, hoping that this time their pursuer wouldn't bother them. But as Uncle Bill had said so often, Louie was a bloodhound for following a trail and a bulldog for hanging on to it.

"He never would have found me if you hadn't come to live with me," Uncle Bill lamented, blowing smoke toward the boy.

Exasperated words escaped before Alex could control them. "I didn't want to! I didn't want my parents to . . . "

"I know! I know!" Uncle Bill broke in, pacing the floor and trailing cigarette smoke. His tone softened. "I'm just spouting off."

When the boy didn't reply, Uncle Bill shook his head ruefully. "I should never have listened to those feds! They assured me that with new papers, a new identity, and a different location, it would be as safe as before you came. But they were wrong! Dead wrong!"

Alex still said nothing but watched with growing fear as his uncle continued pacing.

"I should never have testified," he said, more to himself

than to Alex. "That was my first mistake. I could have been like the others and claimed I never saw anything. But no, I let those feds talk me into believing I'd be safe in their witness protection program. And I was . . . until—"

"Don't, Uncle Bill!" Alex leaped up. "Don't say it! I can't stand it!"

Taking a deep breath, the man slowly nodded. He snuffed out the cigarette and returned to the window. After a quick peek out, he faced the boy.

"I know a man in Anchorage who owes me a favor from a long time ago. It's risky going to him, but if I can work something out, we'll go where Louie can't possibly follow us. We'll be safe, at least for the summer."

The idea of moving again made Alex's insides ache, but he knew it was useless to protest.

"Get your things together, Alex," Uncle Bill said firmly. "Be ready to move when I get back from town. And don't talk to anyone while I'm gone. Hear me?"

Alex nodded and watched in utter hopelessness as his uncle cautiously opened the door, hurried to his car, and drove away.

***

Josh, Tank, and Nathan approached the Ladds' house as Josh glanced curiously toward where the stranger in the big luxury car had driven up Skookum Drive.

"You've got a nice place," Tank observed.

"We like it," Nathan replied, running ahead to remove his shoes at the front door.

"Sure do," Josh agreed, studying the house.

From the front, it looked like a one-story home that faced green mountains rising 4,000 feet less than a quarter mile away. In fact, the house was built into a mountainside, which permitted a lower floor with large windows in each of the three bedrooms on that level.

Each room on the lower floor had sliding glass doors that opened onto a tiny strip of lawn that backed up against a greenbelt*. By lifting his eyes from his bedroom, living room, or kitchen, Josh had a magnificent view of several mountain ranges in the distance.

By dropping his gaze, Josh could look through spruce, cottonwood, and aspen trees and glimpse Skyline Loop.

Josh's reflections were suddenly interrupted by Tank grabbing his arm.

"It's him!"

Thinking Tank meant the stranger who had spoken to Nathan, Josh looked up the hill to where the car had stopped.

"Not that way!" Tank hissed and pointed down the street. "Over there!"

Josh began to turn to his right, but Tank whispered, "Don't look now! Pretend to take off your shoes, then peek."

Josh obeyed, keeping his back toward Skookum Drive but discreetly peering behind as the tires of a gray sedan crunched along the graveled road.

"That's the uncle!" Tank whispered, although there was no way the driver could have heard him. "I've seen his car coming and going from that yellow house."

"You mean where the redheaded—?"

"Exactly," Tank interrupted. "But I don't think the kid was in the car. It looked like just the man by himself."

The boys took off their tennis shoes and stepped inside the house, leaving the door open. Making sure the driver couldn't see them, they watched the sedan turn right and head downhill on Skookum Drive toward the paved road.

Josh and Tank looked at each other, their eyes wide.

"Now's our chance!" Josh exclaimed, starting to put his shoes back on. "Let's try talking to that boy!"

"We'd better wait a couple of minutes," Tank said. "Let's make sure the uncle doesn't come back."

"Right!" Josh straightened up, his shoes retied. Taking them off at the front porch reminded Josh of how they did the same thing in Hawaii. The custom had been introduced there by Asians, who left their shoes outside and changed into slippers. Tank's mother had been especially firm about following that custom because of a white rug she insisted on having in the living room of the Catletts' Hawaiian apartment.

In Alaska, Josh had already learned, some people stepped in from outside and sat down on a small bench to remove muddy shoes or boots. This was especially important during spring "breakup," when the frozen rivers and snow melted, leaving a landscape of mud and slush.

Josh raised his voice. "Mom, I'm back with Tank, but we're going right out again."

"Wait, Josh!" she called from the living room. "You've had enough time off for now. Please finish unpacking those boxes in your room and put things away properly."

"Aw, Mom . . . ."

"Thank you," she said, dragging out the words in a tone that Josh recognized as being final.

Josh and Tank looked at each other and shrugged.

"Another time, I guess," Tank said, reaching for the doorknob. "I'd better get home before my mom and Marsha return."

In his room, Josh stared moodily out the window at the mountains of Chugach State Park*. He was still having trouble learning the difference between Chugach and Chugiak. The small community of Chugiak formed Fireweed's northern boundary as Eagle River did to the south. But right now Josh was focused on the red-haired boy who lived down the street.

I wonder what he meant when I heard him say, 'Nobody can help me,' Josh asked himself. *What is so bad that he wants to run away?*

Josh's thoughts shifted to the mysterious stranger who had asked Nathan about a red-haired boy, but before he could ponder the significance of that, the doorbell rang. "I'll get it," said Josh, hoping Tank had changed his mind and decided to help him unpack.

Instead, when Josh open the door, he blinked in surprise and automatically backed up slightly at the sight of the girl standing there. "Alicia!"

Alicia Wharton shook her head with its pixie haircut of short, yellow strands that clung to her forehead and neck. "Now Josh, you don't have to be afraid of me," she said.

"I've changed since Hawaii."

Trying to hide his embarrassment at his reaction, Josh thought, *I certainly hope so*, but aloud he declared stoutly, "I was just stepping back so you could come in." He turned and called, "Tiffany! Mom! Alicia's here."

"How do you like Alaska so far?" she asked, her gray eyes probing Josh's blue ones.

"Fine, just fine." Josh kept his distance from this 12-year-old tomboy whose reckless spirit had gotten Tank and him into big trouble back on the islands. "Mom! Tiffany!" he called again, backing into the living room.

Alicia removed her shoes and followed, smiling at him. "What makes you think I came to see them?" she asked.

Josh was so startled that he almost tripped over a box waiting on the floor to be unpacked. "Mom?" Josh was almost shrieking while he tried to regain his balance and his dignity. "Tiffany? Where are you?"

The sooner he got away from this slender, outspoken girl, the better. Alicia's mother had died several years before, and her wealthy and indulgent father had given her too much free rein, Josh believed. Her dad had been instrumental in getting the Ladd family to relocate to Alaska, where he and Mr. Ladd were partners in a publishing venture.

Josh sighed with relief when his mother and sister appeared at the sliding glass door from the back deck.

"What's all the yelling about?" Tiffany demanded in her authoritative, big-sister voice. "Mom and I . . . Oh, hi, Alicia."

"Excuse me," Josh said and hurried downstairs to his room, his face flushed. *I'm sure glad she lives in Anchorage instead of on this street where she used to,* he told himself.

He opened a box that needed to be unpacked and tried to focus his thoughts on the red-haired boy. But Alicia had destroyed Josh's ability to concentrate. His mind kept flickering back to her and remembering what a pest she had been in Hawaii. Of course, she now claimed she was changed, but Josh wasn't at all sure of that.

The phone rang and his sister called down that she would get it.

"Josh, it's for you," Tiffany called. "Tank says to hurry."

Josh reached to grab the phone on his nightstand. "Hi. Did the bear come back?"

"No, but something else is in our yard." Tank was excited. "A moose!"

"A real moose?"

"Absolutely!" Tank said. "Marsha's trying to find her camera to get a picture. You want to come look?"

"Sure, if Mom will let me. Call you back."

Josh hung up the phone and raced toward the kitchen, where his mother, sister, and Alicia were unpacking pots and pans from old newspapers.

"Mom, there's a moose in Tank's yard! Can I go see it?"

"May I?" she automatically corrected. "You were over there a little while ago, so you're behind in your unpacking."

"Excuse me, Mrs. Ladd," Alicia said, "but I'd like to go see that moose."

Mrs. Ladd looked surprised. "Why, Alicia, you must

have seen hundreds of them."

"Oh, I have, but this might be a good opportunity to tell Tank and Marsha a few things they need to know about Alaskan wild animals." Alicia stood, wiping newsprint off her hands onto her blue jeans. "I'll be back later."

"Mom, I probably ought to learn that, too!" Josh exclaimed. "Okay?"

Mrs. Ladd sighed. "Oh, I suppose—"

"Mom!" Tiffany broke in. "He's just trying to get out of unpacking! I'm having to do it all!"

Alicia spoke up quickly, "Coming, Josh?"

He glanced at his mother, who nodded and said, "Go ahead. I'll call Tank and tell him you're on your way. And be careful!"

"Any wild animal can be dangerous, including moose," Alicia explained as she and Josh ran side by side toward Tank's house. "A bull moose can have a rack* up to six feet wide. A cow has no antlers, but can strike quickly with her front feet, as well as kick with her hind legs."

Josh glanced over at her, startled.

She paused, then added, "They can trample people to death."

The simple statement caused Josh to run the rest of the way in thoughtful silence.

Tank was waiting at the front door. When he saw Alicia, he frowned, but she seemed not to notice.

"The moose still here?" she asked.

"Yeah." Tank quickly led the way through the house. "Marsha found her camera and is going down the back stairs to get some close-ups."

Josh saw at once that it was a cow that stood nearly five feet at the shoulder. It grazed complacently in the yard, nibbling on some leaves from a high shrub growing in the corner. It ignored the 14-year-old girl who slipped between two slender trees and slowly approached with camera in hand.

Alicia leaned over the railing and called, "Marsha, you're too close."

"It's okay," she called back. "I want to get a good picture." She bent to look into the camera's viewfinder. "It seems so tame. Do you suppose it's a pet?"

"That's no pet!" Alicia's voice had taken on an edge of concern that alarmed Josh. "Please, back up slowly."

"In a minute." Marsha advanced toward the animal, which turned calmly and watched her approach.

Josh's apprehension grew as Marsha moved to within three feet of the moose. Josh whispered to Tank, "I think Alicia's right. She's too close. It's dangerous."

"Aw," Tank scoffed. "Look how gentle that old moose is." He lowered his voice and continued. "Besides, who wants to listen to anything Alicia says? She's always bossy. Remember all the trouble she got us into in Hawaii?"

"Marsha!" Alicia said firmly. "Please! Get away now!"

"One more shot from a lower angle," Marsha called over her shoulder. She dropped to her knees.

Instantly, the moose's right front foot flashed out. Marsha had no time to react before the sharp hoof struck her on the forehead, raked down her cheek and shoulder, and knocked her to the ground.

Josh didn't think; he simply reacted. In one quick leap, he was at the steep, outside stairs, hopping down them two at a time. He was aware that Tank was close on his heels. Marsha was screaming in pain and fright.

Reaching the bottom of the stairs, Josh looked up and saw the moose attempting to trample Marsha. She frantically rolled away, screaming and desperately trying to keep away from the deadly hooves.

"Hey!" Josh shouted, waving his arms wildly and rushing straight at the animal. He was amazed that its shoulder was about the same height as his head. "Hey! Get away! Get out of here!"

The moose calmly regarded him, then abruptly lowered its head.

"Look out!" Tank shouted.

Josh skidded to a halt as the moose charged straight at him!

Chapter Four

A MOOSE ON THE LOOSE

As Josh slid to a stop in front of the charging moose, his heart seemed to stop, too.

Tank shouted, "Look out, Josh!"

Josh was so busy trying to think what to do next that he didn't answer.

The animal ran clumsily, yet it rapidly closed the short distance to the noisy boy who had suddenly fallen silent. Desperately, Josh looked for a way to escape.

Out of the corner of his eye, Josh saw Marsha and was vaguely aware that her screaming had stopped. She was sobbing with fright as Alicia grabbed her arms and backed toward the safety of the house.

Josh leaped aside as the moose rumbled past him, its head lowered. Tufts of grass flew up from its sharp hooves as it pivoted to follow him.

"Get behind a tree!" Tank yelled.

Josh had already decided that was his best option, so he darted toward two slender birch* trees a few feet away. He ducked behind the nearest one, but its narrow four-inch-thick trunk didn't offer much protection. Still, the moose stopped two feet from the other side of the tree and blew noisily through its wide nostrils.

At the same time, Tank rushed close to the animal, shouting, "Hey, old moose! Chase me!"

"No, Tank!" Josh cried as his best friend smacked the animal near its tail, then leaped away.

Instantly, the moose kicked with its hind legs but missed Tank. Then it turned and charged after the boy. He promptly ducked behind the second birch tree's white trunk.

Stopping uncertainly, the cow swung its head from side to side, watching both boys closely.

Alicia called from the back deck, "Don't move, either of you! Maybe she'll get tired and go away. I'm going to call for help."

Josh glanced up. Marsha sprawled across a chaise longue* on the deck with blood on her forehead and cheek.

"How bad is she?" her brother called.

"I don't know," Alicia replied, disappearing into the house.

Marsha said, "I think I'm okay. My head hurts, but the bleeding's stopped. You two be careful."

Tank looked over at Josh. "I've got to help her. See if you can keep this moose busy."

"Wait!" Josh cautioned as the animal slowly started toward the mountains. "I think she's leaving."

The cow, seemingly satisfied that it had showed those boys who was boss, clumsily ambled away toward the forested mountain.

"Whew!" Josh exclaimed as the moose entered the wooded area. "That sure got my blood circulating."

"Yeah. Our first Alaskan adventure."

As the friends hurried toward the house, Josh said, "Thanks for getting that moose's attention off me."

Tank grinned. "You saved my sister, but maybe if I'd thought about it first, I might not have gotten so close."

***

A couple of hours later, Josh and Tank walked down the street, where they met Jacob and his dog.

"What was that ambulance for a while ago?" Jacob asked.

Tank explained what had happened, then concluded, "Marsha's got a big headache and a few stitches on her forehead. But the paramedics said she'll be okay and won't have a noticeable scar."

Josh said, "It surprised me how quickly that moose turned from a contented old cow into a charging freight train."

Jacob speculated, "If Ryan was here, I bet he'd know why the moose attacked your sister."

"That's easy," Tank replied. "It's a wild animal, and my sister should have kept her distance."

Jacob shook his head. "Probably, but I think Ryan would say something like 'When your sister got down low on the ground to get that picture, the moose might have thought she was a wolf, and so it attacked.' Ryan knows just about everything."

"You mean, he thinks he does," Tank corrected.

Jacob defended his friend. "No, he's really very smart. He reads everything and remembers everything. I like him, even though he can be pretty bossy."

"That must be like walking on eggshells," Josh said.

"Sometimes it is."

Josh was intrigued. "Then why are you his friend?"

Jacob shrugged. "He's a good guy when he's not bragging. Besides, my dad says that Ryan is mad because he's so short and can't do anything about it. So he acts important around us kids, and that makes him feel bigger inside."

Tank commented, "That could be, I guess. You must have a smart father."

"Yes, he is smart," Jacob agreed. "Which reminds me, did anybody invite you and your fathers to the dads and sons dinner tonight?"

Tank replied, "There was a notice on the bulletin board outside the grocery store at the mall, so we're going. Well, Josh's father can't make it, but Josh is going with my dad and me."

The boys walked on, passing the yellow house set back from the road. All three eyed it thoughtfully.

"Seems awfully quiet," Josh mused.

"Always does," Jacob assured him.

"Maybe we won't get to talk to Alex until school starts," Tank commented.

"Even then, I won't be able to talk to him," Jacob said.

"Why not?" Josh wanted to know.

"Because I don't go to the public school. I'm home-schooled."

Josh said, "I don't think we know any home-school kids, although I have heard there are a lot of them now."

"Especially here in Alaska," Jacob said.

Josh was intrigued. "Really?"

Jacob nodded. "Some kids who live up on Skookum are home-schooled, but one guy goes to a Christian school. What will you two do?"

"Go to public school," Tank replied. "Always have."

The boys moved to the side of the road at the sound of an approaching car crunching slowly along the gravel.

As the vehicle passed, Josh observed, "Hey, that's the man the redheaded kid called Uncle Bill."

Tank nodded. "He slammed the door in our faces."

The sedan moved on before Josh said thoughtfully, "I feel sorry for that boy. He doesn't seem to have any friends. He must get awfully lonesome."

"We tried to get to know him," Tank reminded him.

Jacob nodded. "So did Ryan and me."

The three boys watched the man park in the driveway, then hurry into the house wearing a hat and dark glasses.

"That's the first time I've seen him leave the car outside," Jacob commented. "He always goes into the garage and closes the door. Sort of mysterious, huh?"

"It's a mystery, all right," Tank agreed.

Josh nodded. "If we could only talk to him—"

"Yeah," Tank interrupted. "But we can't."

"We've got to find a way," Josh said. He again glanced at the yellow house with the closed shades and wondered what was going on inside.

***

Uncle Bill removed his dark glasses before reaching for the blinds. He cautiously peeked out.

"Those nosy kids are still hanging around," he grumbled. Dropping the blinds, he turned to face Alex. "I didn't mean to be gone so long, but I had trouble getting in touch with my contact."

Alex felt his mouth suddenly go dry. He nervously licked his lips, knowing what was coming next.

"You packed?" his uncle asked, taking off his hat and reaching for a cigarette.

Alex wanted to ask, "What is there to pack?" There was just one bag that could fit under an airplane seat or in the overhead compartment. Instead, he forced himself to take a deep breath and say calmly, "I don't want to move again. This is a nice place, and I'm sure those boys—"

"Don't you understand?" his uncle broke in angrily. "This isn't a matter of choice, and it's not just *my* life that's in danger! Louie knows you're with me, so he probably thinks you know everything that happened before you came to live with me."

"But I don't! All I know is what little Dad—"

"I know that," his uncle interrupted again, "and you know that, but Louie doesn't! When are you going to get it through your thick head that he is not a nice man? If he ever catches up with us . . . "

Uncle Bill left the sentence hanging and nervously lit his cigarette.

Alex stood in crushed silence, eyes lowered, hurting from being called thickheaded. He remembered all the name-calling and put-downs he had suffered during the past two months. He wanted to shout his resentment at his uncle, at Louie, and at the terrible problems forced upon him. But hope had trickled away, leaving Alex unsure of anything except that he was miserable, afraid, and terribly lonely.

"I don't really like the idea of spending one more night here, knowing that Louie's in the neighborhood," Uncle Bill said. "But the plane doesn't leave for a couple of days, and I couldn't get a hotel room because it's the height of the tourist season. So we've got to risk staying here again tonight."

What kind of a plane doesn't leave for a couple of days? Alex wondered, but he didn't dare ask.

Uncle Bill added, "I know it's a temptation for you to go wandering in the woods by yourself, especially on these long Alaska days. But you stay inside the rest of the day and hope Louie doesn't find us."

Again, Alex nodded, then headed for his bedroom, thinking, *Sometimes I think it would be best if Louie did find us. At least I wouldn't have to go on like this—scared all the time, moving all the time. . . .*

Then Alex thought of the dark-haired boy who had found him crying in the woods and later had come to the door with his blond friend. *Friends!* He remembered how it used to be, and a dull ache settled on his heart.

***

The sun still sailed high above the mountains surrounding Fireweed when Tank's slender, well-dressed father steered his new pale-blue sedan into the unpaved parking lot of the local community church.

"Looks like we're the first ones here," Tank said.

"Somebody is opening the doors," Josh commented from the backseat.

Mr. Catlett parked the car and got out. "Probably the pastor," he said and strode purposefully forward, his gray suit and tie in sharp contrast to the other man's blue jeans and short-sleeved, open-collar shirt.

Josh and Tank followed at a more leisurely pace across the gravel-covered parking lot. It was easy to see that the grounds had been carved from the forest. A circle of tall trees added natural beauty to the area.

Approaching the church, Josh noticed that it was a simple frame building, unlike the handsome concrete block church in Hawaii where the Ladds and Catletts had memberships.

Instead of Honolulu's colorful explosions of plumeria*, hibiscus*, bougainvillea*, and other flowers around the church, here only a few hardy dandelion plants and white cow parsnips* swayed in the light, cool breeze. The air carried a faint whiff of fried chicken from the church.

"Pastor," Mr. Catlett said as the boys mounted the few steps to the covered entryway, "I'd like to present my son, Tank, and his friend Josh Ladd. Boys, this is Pastor Tom Summers."

They solemnly shook hands while Mr. Catlett explained that Josh's father had wanted to come but had to work late.

"I'm sorry about that, but I'm happy that the rest of you are here," the preacher replied. "Come on in. The others will arrive soon. Ah! There's Richard Gulley with his son, Luke, pulling in now. I'll introduce you."

Luke was nearly as tall as Josh and Tank but was slender and wiry with a thatch of thick, black hair that flopped over his brown eyes.

"You must be the new guys who moved in down the street," he said, smiling warmly after they were introduced. Luke led the way into the main building.

"I live on Sourdough Street," Josh explained. "Tank lives on Clouds Rest."

"I'm on Skookum." Luke swept a hand in a broad gesture around the room. "Someday this will be our fellowship hall—when we build a sanctuary. For now, it serves as the entire church."

Josh and Tank looked around the room, which was plain with a raised platform in back, flanked by the American and Christian flags. A simple wooden cross graced the back wall above a small window. Through it, Josh saw treetops swaying in the breeze.

Instead of comfortable pews as in Hawaii, this church was filled with long tables and chairs. Four women busily set out silverware beside paper plates.

"We Alaskans like to do things for ourselves," Luke said. "We built this place. I helped. Everyone did."

"It's nice," Josh commented.

"It'll get nicer. On Sundays, we move the tables out to make room for folding chairs. But like I said, someday we'll have pews and build a regular, bigger church." Luke glanced toward a small side room with a wide counter. "All those good smells from the kitchen are driving me crazy. Let's go outside until the others arrive."

Josh and Tank followed him to the front steps. Luke said, "You guys should come to church next Sunday at 9:30. We have a great bunch of guys from the neighborhood. You want to come?"

"Hadn't thought about it," Josh confessed. "It'll be the first Sunday in Alaska for Tank and me. We'll have to see where our parents want to go."

Tank looked back to where his father was smiling and talking with the pastor. "I think my dad might be willing to try here," Tank said.

Josh thought of something that made him change the subject. "You said you live on Skookum?"

"Sure do. First house on the right after the curve."

With a meaningful look at Tank, Josh asked Luke, "Did you by chance see a stranger in a big, black car drive on your street today?"

"Yes. He asked me if I knew where a redheaded kid lived. Why do you ask?"

Josh didn't answer Luke's question. Instead, he asked, "What did you tell him?"

"I told him I'd heard that a redheaded kid had recently moved into the yellow house on Clouds Rest Street. Why?"

Josh and Tank exchanged glances before Josh told Luke, "I just have a bad feeling about it."

"You do? Why?"

Josh shook his head. "I really don't know, but ... "

He left the thought unfinished, suddenly concerned about Alex and what kind of trouble he might be in.

***

Alex hadn't been able to sleep. It wasn't his uncle's heavy snoring that kept the boy awake. He could not get used to Alaska's long June daylight hours. His uncle had read in the paper that there would be 19 hours and 21 minutes of daylight every day for the rest of the week.

Last night, from his bedroom window, Alex had seen the sun set at 18 minutes before midnight. Two days from now, June 21, would be the summer solstice*—the longest day of the year. Sunrise would be at 4:21 in the morning.

Not much darkness, Alex fumed. *How can I sleep when night doesn't come?*

It wasn't likely he would have slept anyway. He had too much on his mind. He tried to be grateful for Uncle Bill providing food and shelter, even if he always said harsh things, moved a lot, and didn't allow Alex to have any friends.

But I'm just a kid, Alex thought bitterly. *What can I do?*

He covered his face with his pillow in an effort to blot out some of the light that filtered through the shades. Suddenly, he threw off the pillow and sat up. *What was that noise?*

He strained to hear if it would come again, but he heard only Uncle Bill's snores in the next room and a dog barking in the distance.

Just when Alex started to relax, he heard it again. *What is that?* he asked himself, heart hammering in sudden fear. *It sounds like . . . It is!*

The back door slowly squeaked open.

Chapter Five

MIDNIGHT INTRUDER

With his heart pounding wildly, Alex sat upright in bed, stiff with fear. *Louie's found us!*

The back door did not squeak again, momentarily tempting the boy to think he had imagined it. But he knew the truth. Louie was silently slipping through the house.

Alex sat frozen in fright, listening for any clue to where Louie might be at that moment. Then he realized Uncle Bill was still snoring, blissfully unaware of what was happening. Alex abruptly pushed back the covers as quietly as possible. His bare feet touched the floor, and in two quick steps, he was at his open bedroom door. Cautiously, he peered down the hallway.

In the strange Alaskan half-light somewhere around three in the morning, Alex could see well enough to know that nobody was in the hallway. Then he heard a chair scrape on the kitchen floor. The intruder must have bumped it!

Rising on tiptoes, Alex ran down the carpeted hallway to his uncle's room. Slipping to the side of the bed, Alex

47

urgently whispered, "Uncle Bill! Wake up!"

Fear had tightened Alex's throat so that the words came out as a feeble squeak. Gulping and leaning closer, he tried again, louder. "Uncle Bill! Louie's in the house!"

"Huh?" Uncle Bill grunted sleepily.

Alex repeated his hoarsely whispered warning.

The groggy man reacted instantly. He leaped out of bed just as a footstep was heard at the open door.

Alex whirled around to see a shadowy figure in the semidarkness. Something white flew past Alex's head.

The object struck the intruder in the face. He made a startled but muffled exclamation before the white object fell to the floor. Then Uncle Bill yelled wildly and leaped past Alex to grapple with the trespasser.

The force of Uncle Bill's charge knocked Louie backward so hard that he crashed against the wall in the hallway. The breath was knocked out of him, like a small explosion.

"Get him, Uncle Bill!" Alex cried as the two men struggled in the hallway. "Get him! Get him!"

Alex ran to help, almost tripping over something soft on the floor. Realizing it was Uncle Bill's pillow that had been thrown at the attacker, Alex scooped it up. He ran down the hall toward the living room, following the men as they grappled and fought. Frantically trying to think of some way to help his uncle, Alex swung the tattered pillow over his head, sending a few feathers flying through the air.

Suddenly, a snarling, wolflike animal charged through the open back door and leaped on the struggling men. Alex heard a deep growl and snapping teeth, but there was no barking.

The intruder furiously struck at the animal, which turned on him. Leaping up, he ran down the hallway with the shadowy creature snapping at his heels.

Alex's uncle started to follow, then pitched face forward. His head cracked sharply against the wall, then with a soft moan, he collapsed at the entrance to the living room.

"Uncle Bill!" Alex shrieked in terror, dropping the pillow and kneeling beside him on the hallway floor.

Alex heard a crash in the kitchen, more fierce growling, and then silence as the intruder and his pursuer disappeared into the night.

Alex fumbled for the hall light switch. He flipped it on and bent over the fallen man. "Uncle Bill! You okay?"

His uncle slowly rolled over and leaned against the hallway wall before gingerly touching his right hand to his forehead. "I think I'm okay. I tripped and cracked my head." He glanced toward the kitchen. "What was that thing—that animal? Where did it come from?"

"I think it was the neighbor's dog. I've seen it running around loose at night, and I heard it barking outside earlier."

"Whatever it was, it sure scared off Louie."

Greatly relieved, Alex nodded. "It really did."

Getting to his feet, Uncle Bill said, "Louie will be back, and next time we might not be so lucky." He looked at the pillow Alex had carried down the hallway and growled, "What good would it have done to hit him with that?"

"You threw it at him."

"Only to distract him for a second so I could figure out what to do next. Why didn't you grab something heavy and solid?"

The disapproving tone brought back instant hurtful memories. Alex remembered being told many times, *You dumb kid! You can't do anything right!* He took a deep breath, bitterly thinking, *I was trying to help! What if I hadn't awakened? Oh, what's the use? Nothing's changed! Nothing ever will!*

"We can't be here when Louie comes back. Grab your stuff and let's go," Uncle Bill ordered.

"In the middle of the night?"

"Don't argue! There's no time to lose!"

***

Mrs. Ladd entered Josh's bedroom, saying softly, "Josh, it's time to get up." She slid back the draperies that covered the wide sliding door. The sun, already high in the morning sky, filled the room with brightness.

"You wanted to talk to your father before he left for work, remember?" she said.

Josh opened his eyes, then squinted against the light. The fog clearing from his mind, he nodded. "Thanks, Mom. I'll brush my teeth and be right up."

She turned toward the door leading to the stairs, then stopped and looked back at her son across the half-empty packing boxes. "Please try to understand. He's doing the best he can for us. That means working long hours for a while."

"But he's gone so much," Josh protested. "He got here a month ahead of us, and now that we're here, he doesn't seem to have any time to spend with us."

"We're going to church as a family this Sunday."

Josh frowned. "That's not the same thing. Like last night. Every boy was there with his dad, except me. I got tired of trying to explain to everyone why I came with Tank and his father. Dad spends all his time with that old newspaper!"

His mother opened her mouth to reply, but Josh rushed on. "Sometimes I think he loves that paper more than he does me!"

"Josh!" His mother's voice carried shock and disbelief. "That's unfair!"

"It's true, Mom! I think ... " He broke off as his father's footsteps sounded on the stairs.

John Ladd entered the bedroom. A broad-chested, six-feet-tall man with dark, wavy hair, he was handsome in a gray suit, although there were circles under his blue eyes.

"I'm sorry, son," he said, approaching the bed. "I couldn't help but overhear you. It hurts more than I can say for you to think that."

Upset and embarrassed that his father had heard his outburst, Josh said nothing.

His father sat down on the edge of the bed and looked at Josh with hurt in his eyes. "I'm sorry about not having time to spend with you and the rest of the family. I'm especially sorry about last night, but it couldn't be helped. I love all of you with my whole heart. I would much rather have us all spend time together. But in order to support us, I've got to make this newspaper successful. Do you understand?"

In a vague way, Josh did, but he remembered painfully how he had felt last night—being the only boy without a dad at the father-son dinner. Finally, he said, "I'll try, Dad."

"Good." Lightly touching the boy's hand, Mr. Ladd stood. "Just as soon as I can, I won't work evenings or Saturdays, and we'll make up for lost time. All right?"

"How about the fishing trip?"

"I'm still hoping we can do that, son."

Josh nodded. "Thanks, Dad." He watched his father as he headed for the stairs.

His mother looked sad but managed a smile for Josh before she turned and walked up the stairs ahead of her husband.

Josh stared after them, trying to sort out his feelings. Suddenly, the phone rang. "I'll get it!" Josh called and scooped up the receiver from his nightstand.

"Josh!" Tank's excited voice came over the wire. "He's gone!"

"Who's gone?"

"The redheaded kid! He's moved!"

"What?"

"I went down the street a few minutes ago and saw that their door was wide open. I peeked inside, and there's nothing there except a few pieces of furniture. Some of it's been knocked over, like maybe there was a fight or something."

"You sure?"

"Meet me there and see for yourself."

"I'll get dressed and be right there."

Deeply concerned, Josh slipped into his clothes and dashed toward the kitchen. His parents stopped eating breakfast and looked at him with questions in their eyes.

"Dad, Mom, that was Tank on the phone. I've got to meet him right away."

His father said, "You've got to finish helping unpack. ... " His voice trailed off as his wife gently laid her hand on his.

"What is it, Josh?" she asked.

After recounting the phone call, Josh concluded, "So I want to go down and see the house for myself."

Josh's sister walked in, catching the last part of his explanation. She broke off a yawn to say, "Oh, sure, you're just trying to get out of helping like you did yesterday."

Trying not to show his annoyance, Josh declared, "That's not it." Then seeing the doubt in Tiffany's eyes, he added, "I wasn't going to say anything, but I heard the red-headed boy crying."

Josh hurriedly told about overhearing the boy talking to himself. "I heard the boy, Alex, say, 'Uncle Bill doesn't want me, and I don't want to be here. I should run away.' When I asked if he was okay, he told me to leave him alone, that nobody could help. Then he ran off."

Mrs. Ladd said, "I wish you had told us that at the time."

Tiffany asked doubtfully, "Are you sure you're not making this up?"

Mrs. Ladd said gently, "Josh wouldn't do that."

Josh gave his mother a quick, grateful smile, then hesitated before saying, "There's something else." He took a quick breath and told about the stranger in the big, black car asking Nathan if he had seen a red-haired boy in the neighborhood.

Mr. Ladd declared with a frown, "I don't like the sound of that at all." He pushed back his partially eaten food and quickly stood. "I don't suppose you heard this Alex mention who the man might be?"

"No. No name was mentioned."

"Come on, son," Mr. Ladd said. "I'll go with you to see that house."

When Josh and his father arrived at the yellow house, Tank was waiting at the door with Ryan and Jacob. After Josh introduced his father to the two boys, Ryan announced in his self-confident way, "It's obvious that somebody broke in. I've already called the police."

Images of the mysterious driver in the big, luxury car flashed in Josh's head.

Still standing on the porch, Ryan added, "And there was a fight."

Mr. Ladd asked, "What makes you think that?"

"I'll show you." Ryan motioned for them to follow.

Josh glanced at Tank, who rolled his eyes in disapproval of Ryan's know-it-all demeanor.

"All right, we'll go in," Mr. Ladd said, "but nobody touch *anything*. If something bad did happen here, the police will want to investigate."

Ryan, Mr. Ladd, and Jacob walked through the front

door and across to the living room, with Tank and Josh following behind.

Ryan explained as he walked briskly ahead, "You can see the lights are on, and the blinds are pulled shut over the front window."

Josh passed an old sofa in front of the window, then a tattered recliner. They were obviously inexpensive and in poor condition.

"Obviously, they were in a big hurry," Ryan announced, pointing to a single man-sized sock on the carpet where the hallway began. Three sheets of blank paper lay scattered on the dining room floor. "Looks like the person who dropped them was rushing so fast he didn't stop to pick them up."

From the living room, Josh could see daylight streaming into the kitchen through the open back door. A chair lay overturned on the linoleum.

"Is that what makes you think there was a fight?" Mr. Ladd asked Ryan, not convinced by the boy's detective work.

"There's more—something in the hallway. But first, look at this back door."

When everyone had gathered around, Ryan pointed to the doorjamb. "See where it was pried? Those marks are fresh. Popped open with a bar of some kind, I think. Only took a couple of tries, so there probably wasn't a lot of noise."

Josh watched his father solemnly inspect the broken lock, then nod. "Looks that way to me, Ryan. But what makes you think there was a fight?"

"See for yourself." Ryan led the way to the first bed-room. "It started here."

Tank asked doubtfully, "How do you know that?"

"To someone observant, it's plain enough," Ryan replied, and reconstructed the scene as he imagined it. "Whoever it was that broke in must have been standing at this doorway when the man in the bed rushed him."

Josh said, "The man called Uncle Bill."

Ryan nodded. "That's right."

"How do you figure that?" Tank challenged.

Ryan pointed to the hall wall directly across from the open bedroom door. "See this broken plaster? He got shoved back so hard that he broke it. Then they struggled in the hallway. See how the rug's been ripped? Must have been done by whoever broke in because he was wearing shoes. The other guy was, of course, barefooted when he jumped out of bed."

Josh saw his father's eyebrows arch in admiration, and Josh grudgingly admitted to himself that what Ryan said made sense.

"The two men struggled down the hallway," Ryan continued, walking backward. "Somehow, there was a pillow involved. See the feathers scattered around? The fight ended here. There's blood near the end of the hallway."

Josh joined his father and the other boys in leaning close to examine the red smear on the baseboard.

"Couldn't have been too serious," Mr. Ladd decided after carefully checking the walls and carpet in the hallway, then moving into the kitchen. "No blood on the linoleum or anywhere else."

"No," Ryan admitted. "But it was apparently enough. I can't tell which person was hurt, but the intruder ran out the way he'd come in. Then this Uncle Bill and the red-headed kid packed up real fast and left in the middle of the night. Take a look at both bedrooms and you'll see that."

Mr. Ladd shook his head. "Everything you said seems logical, Ryan."

"I know," he replied smugly. "And I'm sure when the police get here, they'll agree that I'm right."

As Ryan walked toward the back door to examine the doorjamb again, Josh and Tank exchanged looks. Tank threw out his chest, thrust his chin forward, and quietly mimicked Ryan's words. "'I'm sure they'll agree that I'm right.'"

Jacob spoke for the first time. "What do you suppose happened to that redheaded kid?"

Josh admitted, "I was wondering that myself."

"I don't think any real harm was done," his father said thoughtfully, slowly turning to review all the signs. "Whoever broke in probably scared the uncle and the red-haired boy enough that they left hurriedly."

"But where did they go?" Josh wanted to know, wondering if he would ever see the boy again.

Mr. Ladd shook his head. "I don't know, but hopefully they're safe now."

Joining the others again, Ryan disagreed. "I'm not so sure. It all depends on how determined the man is who's after them."

"Yes, Ryan," Josh's father agreed. "You're right. But they're gone, and we'll probably never see them again. Anyway, I'm glad you called the police. They'll follow up on it."

Josh wondered how determined the intruder had been. The thought made Josh shudder, and he suddenly wanted to see the redheaded boy again—before it was too late.

Chapter Six

LOUIE'S ON THE TRAIL

Two nights later, Josh awoke and glanced at the glowing red numbers on his nightstand clock. They read 3:15. *It's June 21, longest day of the year*, Josh thought. *Nearly 20 hours of daylight.*

Josh slid out of bed and padded in his bare feet to the sliding glass door. He pulled the draperies back and looked out. It had been cool and overcast yesterday, but now the sky was clear except for a few clouds on the horizon above the mountains.

It was still light outside—like dusk would be in Hawaii or California, Josh thought. The sun had been down only about three and a half hours, and it would rise in another hour or so. Josh shook his head in wonder.

Standing at the door with the draperies in his hand reminded Josh of Alex peering out from behind the blinds at the yellow house. As Josh returned to bed and began drifting off to sleep, the thoughts kept turning over in his mind. *What happened to him? I hope he's all right, wherever he is.*

The sound of the doorbell's three-note chimes awakened

Josh. He glanced at the clock. "Oh, it's 6:00," he grumbled to his little brother. "Now who could that be at this time of morning? Nathan, I said who could that be?"

When there was no answer, Josh looked across the room and realized he was alone. For the first time in his life, he didn't share a room with Nathan, and it took a little getting used to. Like their sister, the brothers now had their own downstairs bedrooms.

Josh turned over, hoping to go back to sleep. He heard his mother's quick footsteps overhead, moving toward the door. A moment later, Josh listened as the door opened and a man's voice filled the rooms above him. Josh tried to identify whose voice it was, but he couldn't.

Then he heard a girl speaking, and he recognized the voice. *Alicia Wharton, and that must be her dad. But why so early?*

The three voices faded, and Josh knew they had entered the living room. Curiosity made Josh roll out of bed and quickly brush his teeth before pulling on jeans and a T-shirt. Carrying his shoes and socks, he climbed the stairs and entered the living room, passing under the antlered head of a caribou, which had been left by the last occupant of the house.

Josh's slender, dark-haired mother smiled, causing the dimple in her left cheek to show. "Oh, Josh," she said, "I was just telling Mr. Wharton and Alicia that I'm sorry they missed your father. He's gone to work."

He's always working, Josh thought bitterly, then brushed the thought aside to look at the two guests. "Hi," he said to them.

Trent Wharton and his daughter sat together on the sofa facing Mrs. Ladd, who was sitting in a big chair. Looking out the huge picture window behind them, Josh was surprised to see the sky was overcast and a light rain was falling. He recalled a local saying, "If you don't like Alaska's weather, wait a few minutes and it'll change."

Mr. Wharton looked casual and unpolished in his faded blue jeans and red, short-sleeved shirt.

"Sorry to disturb you so early, Josh," he said easily, stretching his legs so the pants pulled up to show tan cowboy boots. "Me and Alicia had to be out this way, so we decided to drop by."

He paused, a smile touching his lips as though he was pleased about something. From under sandy-colored hair, his steely gray eyes fixed on Josh in a way that made the boy think Mr. Wharton could see right through him.

"Where I come from," he continued, "we didn't have phones, so I never got used to calling. Not a lot of phones in Alaska's Bush* either, so I just drop in on folks. We get up early in the flying business."

"It's okay," Josh assured him. "I want to do a lot of things today because of all the daylight we'll have."

Alicia smiled, her eyes bright. She was bursting with some kind of news. "Wait until you hear why we came!" she exclaimed.

"I'm listening," Josh replied, sitting down on the floor beside his mother's big chair and pulling on his socks. Josh had the thought that Mr. Wharton didn't look like a highly successful businessman.

Beginning as a bush pilot*, he now owned floatplanes* as well as fishing and hunting lodges throughout Alaska's vast wilderness area. He was also Mr. Ladd's silent partner.

Mr. Wharton said, "Your dad tells me he's been promising you and your friend Tank a fishing trip."

Josh nodded but didn't reply. That trip looked as if it would never happen, because his father was working day and night, six days a week.

Alicia excitedly blurted out, "What Daddy's trying to say is that we want to take all of you on that trip."

"We?" Josh repeated, trying not to let his alarm show. In her brief Hawaiian visit, Alicia had insisted on doing everything Josh and Tank did. Both boys resented having a girl tag along, even if they did feel sorry for her because she had no mother.

"Yes," Alicia replied. "You, Tank, and your fathers will be our guests for a week. We'll fly in to one of Daddy's lodges. He says it's to reward your father for the hard work he's doing on the paper."

"That's right," Mr. Wharton agreed. "As the silent partner, I put up the money, but only your father has the practical know-how to make the paper work. He deserves a little rest, and Alicia thought it would be great for all of us to go together."

So it was her idea, Josh thought with a tinge of uneasiness. The trouble she had gotten Tank and him into back in Hawaii was fresh and painful in Josh's mind.

"Uh, that's very nice of you," he began uncertainly, "but Dad's probably not going to be able to get away for a while. I can't go without him."

"Oh, he'll go," Alicia declared confidently. "Won't he, Daddy?"

"I wouldn't be surprised." He gave his daughter a quick pat on her forearm. "You're quite a girl."

I've heard that before, Josh thought. His mind flashed back to the Whartons' visit to Hawaii. Josh remembered Mr. Wharton proudly telling Tank and him, "She's still a tomboy, but she'll outgrow that." Then he had added, "Where I was raised before moving to Alaska, we'd say that Alicia is part alligator and part girl." Josh also remembered with a smile that Tank had later confided, "She's more alligator than girl."

Josh was roused from his memories by Mr. Wharton tugging on his cowboy boots and standing.

"Now, Alicia, we had better skedaddle so these folks can get on with their day. I'll call Tank's father, but Josh, we'd be obliged if you told Tank right away."

Josh's mixed feelings churned inside. He was glad that his father's partner was apparently able to get him to do what the boy could not. On the other hand, he didn't relish the idea of having Alicia tagging along on a fishing trip.

Mrs. Ladd stood, following the visitors to the door. "That's thoughtful of you both. My husband has been working very hard, so I will be glad to see him take a little time off, especially with Josh."

"It's a pleasure, Mary," Mr. Wharton assured her.

"Be ready in a couple days," Alicia told Josh. "You

won't need any fishing tackle, but you'd better bring some mosquito repellent."

With a wink at his daughter, Mr. Wharton said, "Josh, I know you've heard we have lots of mosquitoes in Alaska. But it's not true that they're big enough to carry off airplanes to feed their young."

"Oh, Daddy!" Alicia exclaimed with an appreciative titter. "Let's get back to the plane. I've got to do some repair work on it."

After they had gone, Josh stood frowning at the door. In Hawaii, Alicia had claimed that her father let her take the plane's controls even though she was too young to solo. She also boasted of working on her father's aircraft, but Josh didn't feel comfortable with the idea of flying in one that she had tinkered with.

"I'd better let Tank know," Josh told his mother.

"It's too early," she reminded him. "Come have some breakfast and tell me more about this red-haired boy."

It was good to talk about it, Josh realized as he sat at the kitchen table and told her everything he knew. His mother made his favorite—pancakes—and listened without comment until he had finished.

"I can't explain it, Mom, but I feel awful about him. He needed a friend, yet he wouldn't let me be one."

"Sounds to me as though his uncle was the one who wouldn't let him have friends." She flipped a pancake in the frying pan, showing that it was a perfect golden brown, just the way her son liked them.

"He was in big trouble, Mom, and I couldn't help."

"You tried. Now he's gone. All we can do is pray for him, wherever he is."

Later, Josh phoned Tank to report on the Whartons' invitation, and he reminded his friend that this was the longest day of the year. "So let's make the most of it," he suggested. "Want to go exploring around here?"

"Sound's great," Tank replied. "Where do you want to start?"

"How about just beyond your own backyard?"

Tank hesitated. "Are you forgetting the bear and moose that made themselves at home there?"

"No, but it stands to reason that all the kids who live around here—like Ryan, Jacob, and Luke—must explore these hills and woods all the time. Let's ask them if it's safe."

"Better just ask Jacob or Luke," Tank suggested. "If you ask Ryan, he'll tell you more than you want to know."

Josh agreed and made plans to meet Tank later. As he prepared to leave, his mother insisted that he put on at least a light jacket to fend off the rain. A few minutes later, Josh's knock on Jacob's front door sent Willi into a fury of barking as the dog charged through the house and jumped against the closed door. When Jacob opened the door, Willi's behavior totally changed. He whined excitedly and wagged his tail in recognition.

"Hi, Jacob," Josh said. "I have a question."

"Sure, come on in."

"No thanks. I'm on my way to Tank's house. We want to go exploring around here, but we want to be sure it's safe. How do we keep from getting lost, and what about bears, moose, and other animals?"

"Bears and moose are about the only thing you have to watch out for. So us guys carry pepper spray for protection against them."

"Pepper spray? Isn't that what some policemen carry to subdue criminals and suspects who get violent?"

"I don't know about that, but around here, we carry it to protect against bears. Wait a minute and I'll show you."

Jacob left Josh standing on the porch for a minute, then returned with an orange-colored can about six inches long.

Josh listened in fascination as the usually quiet Jacob explained in detail how the canister worked.

When he had finished, Josh said, "Hey, why don't you bring that and come with Tank and me? You can show us all the neat places there are around here."

"I can't. Dad drove to the repair shop to have a mechanic check a strange noise in the motor. If the mechanic can fix it, my parents will be driving into Anchorage to do some shopping, and I've got to go with them. But since I'm not going to need the pepper spray today, why don't you take it?"

"Uh, no thanks," said Josh, who had lost his enthusiasm for exploring unfamiliar territory, since pepper spray was necessary as a defense against wild animals. He also knew that he should get permission from his parents, since they probably hadn't heard about the protection some neighborhood kids carried.

"I think Tank and I will wait until we can go with you

or some of the other guys from around here."

"Sounds good," Jacob replied. "Well, have fun, whatever you do."

A few minutes later, Tank met Josh at the front door. Josh repeated everything Jacob had said.

Still in the doorway, Tank shook his blond hair in wonder. "I'm beginning to think that Hawaii's sharks, Portuguese men-of-war*, moray eels*, and sea urchins* aren't as dangerous as the creatures living here. But let's not tell our mothers that."

From the living room, Mrs. Catlett asked in her low, musical voice, "What's that you're not going to tell us?"

Tank rolled his eyes and whispered, "Mothers! They not only have eyes in the backs of their heads, but they have ears everywhere."

Josh grinned at his friend and walked into the Catletts' living room. Like the Ladd home, most of the boxes had been unpacked, although the pictures hadn't been hung yet. Mrs. Catlett looked up from where she had been sitting on the sofa. She was a pretty woman of medium height with ash-blonde hair and green eyes.

"Before I start putting up these pictures," she said, gesturing toward some leaning against the walls, "why don't you tell me what you weren't going to tell your mothers?"

Josh and Tank exchanged glances. When Tank shrugged, Josh explained what Jacob had told him.

"Goodness! Pepper spray!" Mrs. Catlett exclaimed when he finished. "I had no idea. Tank, you know your father and I wouldn't want you going into those woods until we've had a chance to check with other neighborhood parents."

Tank protested, "Aw, Mom . . . "

"I suspect both you boys secretly would rather we did that anyway," she said.

When they smiled, Mrs. Catlett instructed, "I think you boys had better find something else to do today instead of exploring the woods. And you'd better do it before I think of some things Tank could do to help around here."

Tank turned toward the door. "We're on our way."

"To where?" his mother asked. When the friends hesitated, Mrs. Catlett said, "Now might be a good time to get better acquainted with the other boys in the neighborhood. Find out what *they're* going to do on this long day."

"Good idea," Josh agreed.

"Just let us know where you are," Mrs. Catlett said. "Call us and give us the number where you are. We can start making a list of all the phone numbers of other children in the neighborhood."

The boys agreed and rushed out of the house into a gentle drizzle. As they started down the street, Josh suddenly stopped and grabbed his friend's arm.

"Look!" He pointed toward the long driveway leading to the secluded yellow house. A big, black car was rapidly backing up. "That's the same one we saw before, and that's got to be the same man driving, too!"

The car reached the gravel street and rapidly accelerated

downhill, throwing gravel behind it.

Tank said, "Yeah, and he sure is in a hurry."

As the vehicle turned left from Clouds Rest onto Sourdough, Josh commented, "He must have seen that Alex and his uncle have taken off and he's angry."

"He found where they lived, but it's too late."

"Yes," Josh said thoughtfully, "but where did Alex go? And why does that man keep after him?"

The questions haunted Josh as he and Tank continued down the hill.

BASEBALL UNDER THE MIDNIGHT SUN

Josh and Tank turned left onto Sourdough Street and met Jacob and Ryan coming toward them with Willi. The big malamute rushed up, barking furiously, then almost twisted himself in half when Josh and Tank petted him.

"Hi, Ryan," Josh said as the four boys met. "Hey, Jacob, I thought you were going to Anchorage with your parents."

"I was, but the mechanic said Dad's car isn't safe to drive that far until it's repaired. So I went over to Ryan's."

"Where are you two going?" Josh asked.

"No place special," Ryan replied, then quickly added, "Did you see that big, black car go zipping by?"

Josh nodded. "We saw him backing out of that place where Alex and his uncle lived."

"There's something spooky about all this," Jacob said. "What do you guys make of it?"

Before Josh or Tank could answer, Ryan declared, "It doesn't matter now. They're gone, and I'm glad. I don't like weird people living in our neighborhood."

Recalling his first encounter with Alex, Josh ventured,

"Maybe they aren't weird."

"What would you call them?" Ryan demanded sharply.

Sensing that Ryan didn't like to be challenged, Josh kept his voice casual but still tried to make his point. "I don't know about the uncle, but I think Alex is a boy who is in some kind of trouble, and it's not his fault."

"Oh, you do, huh?" Ryan snapped. "What makes you think that?"

Out of the corner of his eye, Josh noticed that Jacob took a deep breath and lowered his head as though he was uncomfortable with Ryan's sharp tone. For a moment, Josh thought of telling about seeing Alex alone, crying and talking to himself. But Ryan's attitude made Josh decide that he would not discuss the obvious anguish he had seen in his first brief encounter with Alex.

"Just call it a hunch if you want," Josh quietly replied, then quickly retreated from the sensitive subject. He asked, "What do you guys do on a long day like this?"

Ryan seemed satisfied that he had dominated the conversation, and his voice softened. "Oh, lots of things."

"Yes," Jacob agreed, "but tonight, we have our midnight softball game."

"Midnight?" Tank's voice held surprise.

"Sure," Ryan quickly replied. "I'm the pitcher, but you guys can play outfield if you want."

"We got the idea from Fairbanks," Jacob explained. "There they have the Midnight Sun Baseball game for the whole town. But here, we just have neighborhood kids and a few of our friends from Eagle River, Chugiak, and sometimes a few come from Anchorage."

Ryan added, "Anchorage has the Mayor's Midnight Sun Marathon, but who wants to fight those crowds?"

Jacob nodded. "So we celebrate the longest day of the year with a neighborhood ball game. Remember, the sun won't set until almost midnight."

"I've played under electric lights on the field," Tank admitted, "but never after midnight and never where it doesn't seem to get dark all night."

"Oh, it'll get dark this winter," Ryan assured him. "For months, we'll have the longest nights imaginable. So we enjoy the long days while we can. Now, do you guys want to come tonight?"

"Sounds like fun," Josh admitted. "But that's past my bedtime."

"Mine, too," Jacob assured him, "but most parents make an exception for this one night. Besides, most of them are there to cheer their kids on."

"I go to bed when I want," Ryan announced proudly just as a car crunched onto the road behind them and headed toward the Ladds' driveway.

All four boys turned to look.

Ryan slapped his forehead with an open palm. "Oh, no! It's that tomboy who used to live down the street."

Josh suppressed a smile, knowing that Alicia and Ryan were certain to cause sparks, because they were both opinionated and strong-willed.

Jacob said, "She always plays in our game, but she wants to pitch."

"I'm better than she is," Ryan declared as the car Alicia was riding in turned into the Ladds' driveway. "But because it's a neighborhood rule that everybody gets to play, she gets in—and always loses, too."

Josh saw Jacob silently mouth words, and he was sure they were, "No, she doesn't."

"We've got to go talk to her," Josh announced, watching the girl and her father get out of the car. "See you guys later."

"At the game?" Jacob asked.

"Probably so," Tank answered, falling into step beside Josh. Then he continued under his breath, "Boy, Ryan sure is touchy! I hope we're not going to have to watch every word we say around him."

"Me, too," Josh agreed, waving to Alicia and her father.

When everyone had gathered in the Ladds' living room, the Whartons explained that they had a firm date for the fly-in fishing trip.

"When?" Josh asked eagerly.

"Next Monday," Mr. Wharton replied. "Think you boys and your fathers can make it?"

"Mine can," Tank said, "although he may not be able to stay more than a couple of days."

Josh felt his stomach tighten with doubt. "I don't know about my dad yet."

"Call him and find out," Alicia suggested.

Mrs. Ladd shook her head. "He doesn't like to be disturbed at work. There will be plenty of time to ask him this evening." Catching her son's crestfallen look, she hastily added, "Let's go on faith that my husband can make it.

What preparations are necessary, Trent?"

"I brought a list, Mary." Mr. Wharton handed it to her, explaining, "John will need a fishing license, but Josh and Tank won't because they're under 14. They won't need any tackle either, since we'll provide that, but they will need insulated, chest-high waders."

"John has those, but Josh doesn't."

"Me neither," Tank said.

"In that case," Alicia's father said, "I'll get some for the boys."

Shaking her head, Mrs. Ladd said, "That's very kind of you, Trent, but you're already doing enough. We'll buy Josh's waders."

Tank chimed in, "My dad will buy mine, too."

"Make sure they're insulated," Alicia cautioned. "The water won't be much above freezing."

"Really?" Mrs. Ladd raised her eyebrows. "How much higher?"

"Oh, it's somewhere around 34 degrees."

"My goodness, 32 is freezing!" Mrs. Ladd exclaimed.

Alicia's father chuckled. "Sometimes the water warms up to 36 or 37 before the summer's over."

Josh saw the concern in his mother's eyes. "I'll be careful, Mom. So will Tank."

"I've read about hypothermia*," she said with a frown. "I know there's great danger in Alaska's waters."

Alicia declared, "There's more danger from bears and moose, but—"

"Thanks a lot, Alicia!" Tank exclaimed. "Don't tell that

to *my* mom."

She turned to him, eyes blazing, but Mrs. Ladd spoke first. "Your mother and I will talk this over, Tank, so don't be upset with Alicia."

Josh gave his friend a warning look, and Tank relaxed. Fire faded from Alicia's eyes. "Thanks, Mrs. Ladd."

"Josh, you and Tank got time to drive into Anchorage with us and get those waders?" Mr. Wharton asked.

"You bet!" he answered.

A short time later, Mr. Wharton guided his car down from the mountainside onto Skyline Loop. The paved road wound its way through the mountains to Glenn Highway, which led to Anchorage.

Sitting in the backseat with Tank, Josh could see that his friend was still tense from his brief verbal exchange with Alicia. So Josh looked for a safe subject. "Why do they call this area Fireweed?"

Alicia turned in the front passenger seat to explain. "Fireweed is a tall plant, from two to six feet high, with bright pink blossoms. They only bloom from late June to August, but they're so pretty."

Her father added, "They get their name from their ability to spring up after a fire. That's because they have a deep root system, so the plant survives."

Soon they arrived in Anchorage, which Josh decided looked like any modern city. Mr. Wharton eased through the downtown area of high-rises, heavy traffic, and commercial establishments.

"I like Anchorage," Tank said. "It's really a pretty spot

with all that water on one side and the mountains on the other."

Alicia nodded. "That's Knik Arm ahead and the Chugach Mountain Front behind us. It really is a pretty area. But have you seen pictures taken after the big earthquake?"

When both boys said no, Alicia continued. "We've got a book you should see. Right, Dad?"

"Right. It happened about 5:00 the afternoon of Good Friday, 1964. It was the most devastating North American earthquake in history, registering 9.2 on some seismographs*."

Josh leaned forward in the backseat. "I heard about it from my dad. He said that earthquake was twice as big as the 1906 San Francisco quake."

"We have a lot more earthquakes here than California does," Alicia said with what seemed to Josh a combination of pride and fear. "We've got 35 active volcanoes and 21 dormant ones."

Josh whistled in amazement.

Slowing the car, Mr. Wharton swept his hand from right to left as he said, "This whole area was destroyed by the '64 quake. We're on Fifth Street, which was part of a 30-block area that was heavily damaged. But Fourth Street collapsed from four to 10 feet below where it had been moments before the quake hit."

Tank looked around. "I don't see any sign of earthquake damage now."

"Of course not." Alicia's tone was abrasive. "It's all rebuilt. Dad, tell them about the landslides and the tidal wave caused by the quake."

"Later," he replied, pulling the car into a parking lot in front of a department store. "Tank, this store that your dad manages was totally destroyed and rebuilt."

"We can get everything we need for the trip right here," Alicia said, flashing a smile.

Tank sounded disappointed as he asked, "You still planning on going, Alicia?"

She gave him a scathing look. "Of course! I bet I'll catch a bigger fish than either of you."

Josh laid a warning hand on his friend's arm. "I hope you do, Alicia."

"Thanks." She rewarded him with a big smile and slid out of the vehicle.

Tank muttered under his breath, "Well, maybe you do, but I don't."

"Don't let her upset you," Josh whispered. "Let's just all have fun. Okay?"

"Alicia and Ryan!" Tank said. "What did we do to deserve them?"

It was the first time Josh had seen the multistore building that stretched from the middle of the block all the way from Fifth to Fourth Street. Josh enjoyed the soft chiming of signal bells and the smell of new clothes and leather goods.

As they approached the elevator that would take them to Sam Catlett's office on the top floor, Josh stopped and stared at a sign. It read, "We ship to the Bush."

"Mr. Wharton, what does that mean?"

"Oh, that's a common sign, Josh. It means that if something is bought here but it's to be delivered to a wilderness village, this store will fly it there."

Alicia quickly added, "In Alaska, Bush is always spelled with a capital B. So are Outside and Lower Forty-Eight."

Tank motioned for Josh to hold back as Mr. Wharton and his daughter entered the elevator. Tank whispered, "She sounds like Ryan, always showing off her knowledge."

"Shhh!" Josh answered and entered the elevator.

Tank's father received them warmly, shaking hands with Trent Wharton and smiling at the others. After chatting for a couple of minutes, Mr. Wharton asked to be excused, saying they needed to buy waders for the boys.

Tank's dad said, "My wife called after Josh's mother phoned her, so I've made arrangements to expedite your shopping. Get what you want, and have the salesperson at the register call me when you're ready to leave."

A hour later, Mr. Wharton and the others locked their purchases in the trunk and got back into the car.

"Josh," Mr. Wharton began, "do you want to stop by your father's office for a minute?"

Josh imagined how busy his dad was and felt uneasy about disturbing him, but Alicia spoke up before Josh could.

"Oh, let's do, Daddy. I'd love to see a newspaper being put together."

Tank said, "It's not really a newspaper. It's a periodical—sort of like a magazine."

Alicia twisted in the front seat to give him a cool look. "What's the difference?"

Fearful that Tank would get himself into more trouble with Alicia, Josh decided to answer. "Dad has no presses.

He has an office with people who sell the advertising and others who write the copy, develop the pictures, and lay out the pages. Then what they call flats are taken to the big newspaper, where Dad pays them to make plates and print the paper."

"Just the same, I want to see his office," Alicia declared, "especially since Daddy is part owner."

Entering the office near the landmark Captain Cook Hotel, Josh's eyes swept the large room. Phones were ringing and people were rushing about or sitting at desks with computer screens. The receptionist called Mr. Ladd's office and motioned for Josh and the others to go ahead. Nobody even looked up as the visitors threaded their way through desks and office equipment to a windowed office.

Josh thought his father looked tired as he rose to meet them at the door. His shirtsleeves were rolled up halfway to his elbow, and his collar had been opened and the tie pulled loose.

"What an unexpected pleasure to see all of you," he declared, shaking hands with Mr. Wharton. "Sit down."

"Thanks, John," Alicia's father replied. "We can't stay long. We just dropped by because my daughter has never seen a publication put together."

"Would you like a tour?" Mr. Ladd asked. When Alicia nodded, he said, "I'm bucking a deadline, but I'll get someone to show you around."

Josh suppressed a moan. If his father was this busy, he almost certainly wouldn't be able to go on the fishing trip next Monday.

After a quick phone call, a young woman arrived and received her boss's instructions to give the visitors a tour. On their way out of the office, Josh looked expectantly at his dad.

"I hope to see you tonight, son," he said tiredly. "If I'm late, I'll come in and see if you're still awake."

Choking down his disappointment that his dad might be late again, Josh replied, "Oh, I'll be awake—that is, if I get your permission to go to the big midnight softball game tonight. Alicia's going to play, so is it okay if I go, too?"

Sensing hesitation, Mr. Wharton said, "Actually, the game starts at 10:00 and runs just past midnight. I'll look out for Josh and Tank."

"Thanks, Trent. And son, I'll try to get home in time to watch."

"Sure," Josh said without conviction and followed their tour guide. But his mind wasn't on her words.

Tank dropped back to whisper, "I'm sorry, Josh."

"Does it show that much?"

"I can see the hurt in your face. But your dad always went places and did things with you in California and then in Hawaii. Just hang on. He'll get caught up here pretty soon, and it'll be like old times."

Josh nodded halfheartedly. "I know, but it doesn't look as if it'll be in time for the fishing trip."

"You can still go."

"It won't be the same without Dad."

Tank didn't answer, suggesting to Josh that his friend agreed.

Suddenly, Josh's thoughts flashed to Alex. *I wonder if he doesn't have a dad. Maybe that's why he lives with his uncle. And maybe his uncle doesn't really want him around and—*

"Hey, snap out of it," Tank said quietly, giving Josh a poke on the shoulder. "You're not paying attention to our guide, and Alicia's looking at you sort of funny."

Taking a deep breath and slowly letting it out, Josh replied softly, "I just have a bad feeling about Alex."

"How so?"

"You and I are friends, and Jacob and Ryan have each other, but Alex has nobody. Well, except an uncle who yells at him. And they're in some kind of danger from that man who's trying to find them."

"If we got mixed up in that situation, that guy could come after *us*. We don't need that kind of trouble."

Josh knew Tank was right, but he couldn't shake the bad feelings about Alex that gripped his heart.

Chapter Eight

WHAT HAPPENED TO ALEX?

That evening, Josh watched in wonder as the sun set at about 15 minutes before midnight. He was so engrossed in the spectacle that he momentarily forgot it was the top of the ninth inning, his Fireweed team was behind three runs to one, and he was standing in the outfield.

That's when he heard the crack of Alicia Wharton's bat and the explosive yelling of the crowd in the bleachers.

"It's yours, Josh! Make it the third out!"

He heard Tank's words in time to look up and see the softball curving down from the sky directly toward him in left field. He reached up with his open mitt, but it was too late. The ball plopped loudly in the dust behind him.

Simultaneously, the visiting fans cheered and the home-team supporters groaned. Josh made a fast recovery and chased down the ball. But in his embarrassment at missing the easy catch, Josh threw wildly. Jacob, playing second, made a valiant leap, stretching high to try to snag the ball, but it sailed over his head and bounced toward first base.

The crowd roared. "Run, Alicia! Keep going!"

She didn't need to be reminded. She rounded first and sprinted for second as Luke Gulley ran after the ball from his position at first base.

When Alicia was safe on second and the crowd had quieted, she smiled and called, "Thanks, Josh!"

From the mound, Ryan turned and yelled angrily, "Watch it, Josh! You let a girl get a double!"

Josh mouthed the words, "I'm sorry." He already knew full well what his error had done. If the next players at bat could drive Alicia home, that would be her second run for the night. It would also put the visitors so far ahead that the Fireweed team's chances of victory would be slim.

From his position in right field, Tank called good-naturedly, "You never saw a sunset before, Josh?"

"Not on a day as long as this," he admitted sheepishly as play resumed.

The light rain had passed by midafternoon, and the game had started at 10:00 under a bright sun. Now, after more than 19 hours of daylight, the low clouds on the western horizon glowed with brilliant hues of purple and gold.

But it wasn't only the unusually long day that distracted Josh. His thoughts jumped between his father's absence and Alex's disappearance.

Mr. Ladd had planned to attend the midnight game with his wife, daughter, and younger son, but an emergency had kept him at the office. There seemed little likelihood that he would be able to leave Monday on a fishing trip, and that troubled Josh.

As for Alex, the police had not found cause for alarm. A man and a boy had left the yellow house in the middle of the night, but there was no concrete evidence of foul play. The case seemed closed. Still, Josh couldn't shake his troubled thoughts about the red-haired boy or his disappointment that his father wasn't at the game.

A stocky boy for the visitors' team hit a hard grounder that sent Alicia scooting toward third base, but Jacob's quick handling of the ball beat the runner to first for the third out.

The home-team supporters cheered and applauded as the Fireweed players headed toward the dugout.

Tank trotted up beside Josh. "Bottom of the ninth," he commented, "but we've still got a chance to win."

Alicia, passing the boys as she headed for the mound, overheard him. "You need two runs to tie us and three to win," she reminded them. "You can't do it."

Tank lowered his voice and mimicked her. "'You can't do it.' Well, let's show her, Josh."

Josh said nothing but hurried toward the dugout, where Ryan waited with anger in his eyes. "You never played ball before, Josh?" he asked sarcastically.

"I've sure played better," he admitted.

"Then see if you can get a hit next time at bat."

Tank gave Josh a friendly pat on the shoulder as they sat down on the bench. "Don't let him get to you—or Alicia either."

Shaking his head, Josh admitted, "I'm trying. But she is a good pitcher. She has more strikeouts than Ryan."

"Yeah! He's steaming mad at her, but Ryan's still determined to win."

Alicia struck out the first batter. The second one got a base hit, the third batter went down swinging, but the next one got a double.

Ryan looked at the runners on second and third before turning to Josh, who was loosening up before his turn at bat. Glaring at him, Ryan said, "Two outs. The tying runs are on base. Now, make up for your error by driving Jacob home from third and advancing Luke to third. If you get on first, then we've got a chance to win with the next batter."

Nodding and focusing his attention on the game, Josh walked to the plate and faced Alicia on the mound. She grinned self-assuredly at him, causing him to clench his teeth. Then he reminded himself, *It's only a game. Still*, he thought, *it would be nice to get a solid hit off Alicia.*

Her first pitch was low and outside. The second was a called strike. The third ball was in the dirt.

Two balls, one strike, Josh reminded himself.

Ryan yelled from the bench, "You've got to hit it!"

Distracted by Ryan's angry tone, Josh heard the ball solidly smack into the catcher's mitt before Josh even realized it had been thrown.

"Strike two!" the umpire called.

The visiting players began a unified, disruptive chatter. "Hey, batter, batter, batter . . . "

Alicia pitched a hard underhanded ball that came so close to Josh that he had to arch his body and jump away to avoid being hit.

When he stepped back to the plate and looked at her, she grinned. *She's just trying to scare me*, Josh told himself.

With a full count of three balls and two strikes, Josh forced himself to put aside thoughts of his father and Alex.

Ryan yelled, "Last chance, Josh!"

As Alicia faced him on the mound for the critical pitch, Josh realized her grin had been replaced by a scowl. He understood her problem. If she walked him, the bases would be loaded. Then, in the unlikely possibility that the next batter hit a triple, it would cost her the game. On the other hand, she could win with one more pitch. A swinging miss or a called strike would cost Fireweed the game and bring Ryan's fury down on Josh.

Alicia wound up and pitched underhand.

Now! Josh thought, and he swung from the hip, strong shoulders putting power into his swing. He felt a satisfying crack as the bat and ball connected. He watched the ball suddenly reverse direction and streak above Alicia's head. With wide eyes, she watched as the ball flew over the second baseman's head. Josh dashed toward first as the crowd went wild.

"Go on! Go on!" Tank's familiar voice sounded above the throng.

Nearing first, Josh saw the right fielder and center fielder running toward each other and the ball arcing down. *If they catch it, the game's over*, Josh told himself. He kept running as fast as he could.

A mighty clamor of disappointment erupted from the visitors' bench and a cheer from the local Fireweed rooters as the outfielders collided and missed the catch. Josh pulled up at third, panting, as the right fielder leaped up and hurled the ball toward second. By then, two runners had crossed the plate.

Standing on third, Josh briefly joined the home team's happy shouts. *Tie score, three and three, with two outs. If I can get home, we'll win. Who's up next?*

Josh smiled with satisfaction and glanced at Ryan, who strode purposefully to the plate. Cupping his hands to his mouth, Josh yelled encouragement. "Bring me home!"

Leading off third, Josh prepared to sprint for the winning run if Ryan got a hit. Alicia suddenly threw to third, forcing Josh back. The third baseman caught the ball but almost dropped it before throwing it back to Alicia.

The crowd, sensing victory or defeat in the next few seconds, kept up a roar until Alicia pitched again.

"Strike one!"

Josh took another lead, whispering, "Come on, Ryan! Get a base hit so I can score!"

"Strike two!"

Josh saw Ryan's face tighten, and Josh knew how Ryan felt. He could lose the game in one more pitch, and that would be hard for him to take.

Or he can win, Josh realized. He again cupped his hands to his mouth and yelled, "You can do it, Ryan!" *And I can help*, Josh thought as he took a couple of quick steps from the bag, keeping a close eye on Alicia.

Instantly, she threw to third. The baseman had to jump high to make the catch. He swung to tag Josh with the ball, but Josh's foot was again safely on the bag.

I think that shook up Alicia, Josh told himself with

satisfaction. *She's a little wild.* When Alicia again had the ball, Josh took another quick leadoff.

Watching Josh out of the corner of her eye, Alicia threw what could have been the third strike and final out. Instead, Ryan connected solidly for a base hit to center field.

"Come on home!" Tank cried, but Josh was already racing toward the plate for the winning run. He saw Ryan was going to beat the ball to first.

It was past midnight but still light on Alaska's longest day of the year as Josh dashed across home plate. The Fireweed team and fans erupted in joyous shouts. "We won! We won!"

***

The next Sunday, Mr. Ladd sat with his family around the dining room table. Josh noticed how tired he looked. He admired his father's commitment to attend church with his family each week, which he had done that morning despite his exhaustion.

"Pastor Summers preached a good sermon, didn't he?" Josh's mother asked as she passed the platter of salmon. Jacob's parents had brought the fish over late yesterday, saying they had caught it earlier that day.

"He really did," Mr. Ladd agreed. "I was glad to hear him talk about how every individual is valuable in God's sight."

Josh ate in silence, bothered by memories of hearing Alex crying and berating himself. Obviously, the red-haired boy didn't have a high opinion of himself.

"This fish is delicious!" Tiffany exclaimed. "Dad, you did a great job barbecuing it."

Nathan, with his mouth full, showed his appreciation by nodding enthusiastically.

"Thanks," Mr. Ladd replied, managing a tired smile.

"Speaking of fish," Josh said, looking to the head of the table where his father sat, "are you going to be able to go fishing tomorrow?"

Josh sensed bad news when his mother and father exchanged glances. Mr. Ladd turned to his son and sighed. "Sorry, son. I'm really struggling to get this business up and running."

Fighting down his disappointment, Josh told his dad, "Mr. Wharton said you can go. He's your partner."

"That's very kind of him, son, but Trent put up the venture capital for this business. I'm the one who has to make it profitable, and so far, I've not done that."

Josh dropped his fork with a clatter onto the plate. "Are you saying we definitely can't go?"

"I can't go, but Trent graciously volunteered to be responsible for you, and Sam Catlett also said he would look out for you. So you may go."

Scowling, Josh protested, "But I want us to go together, Dad!"

"I didn't say I couldn't go *at all*. I'll try hard to get there before the end of the week, but you'll have to start the trip without me."

***

Early the next morning as Josh was dressing, he thought that he could understand a little of how Alex felt—

lonely and downcast. Alex apparently had no father. Josh assumed that the red-haired boy's parents were dead, although Josh could only guess that's why he had to live with his mean uncle.

Josh climbed the stairs to the kitchen and the hot breakfast his mother had waiting. Through the big dining room window, he could see that another light rain was falling.

Mrs. Ladd explained gently, "Your dad came down to say good-bye before he left for work, but you were asleep."

"He works all the time!" Josh cried.

"He's doing the best he can." Mrs. Ladd placed two large, brown pancakes in front of her son. "Please try to understand."

"I am, Mom! I really am! But this trip is so important! It won't be the same without Dad."

"He wants to be with you as much as you want him to be, and he'll try to join you before the week is out." Mrs. Ladd reached up to the counter and slid a small box in front of Josh. "Meanwhile, he left a gift for you."

Opening the box, the boy stared. "It's a whole bunch of dry flies for fishing. There's a Royal Coachman, a Black Gnat . . . " Josh looked up at his mother with shining eyes. "He remembered I wanted something like this from way back before Hawaii, when we lived in California and he taught me to fly-fish."

"Your father remembers many things. I hope that you'll remember he loves you, even though he can't always be with you. Now, eat your breakfast before Tank and his dad get here."

When Mr. Catlett and Tank picked him up for the ride to Lake Hood near the Anchorage International Airport, Josh was still feeling touched by his dad's thoughtful gift, and he proudly showed it to Tank and his father.

Tank agreed the dry flies were special, then scoffed good-naturedly. "Even so, I predict you'll spend most of your time with your fancy lures caught in the trees or brush while I pull out big lunkers with my old spinning rod and live bait."

"We'll see about that!" Josh exclaimed, rising to the challenge.

Mr. Catlett chuckled from behind the steering wheel. "Our guide might have something to say about the baits you're both planning to use."

"Guide?" Josh repeated.

"Sure," Tank's father replied, slowing as he approached Lake Hood, with its floatplanes of all colors tied up or taxiing for takeoff. "In Alaska, professional guides help fishermen find and catch the biggest fish."

Alicia and her father were on hand to greet Josh, Tank, and Mr. Catlett. As they headed for their plane, Alicia said, "This is the largest and busiest seaplane base in the world. There can be more than 800 takeoffs and landings on a busy summer day."

It was an impressive place, Josh admitted to himself as they were introduced to their pilot, Sven Swensen.

Josh noticed that Alicia smiled a lot at the handsome young pilot and asked him many questions as he stowed their gear in back. "There's plenty of room," he replied to one query. "This aircraft carries six people."

"Will we see Mount McKinley*?" Alicia asked, then quickly added, "you know, it's 20,320 feet high." Turning to look at the boys, she explained, "That's the highest point in North America."

Josh and Tank already knew that, but they just nodded as though it was new information to them.

Sven replied dryly, "No, Alicia, I'm afraid this overcast will hide Denali National Park* and that mountain." He turned to the others. "Get aboard, and we'll be on our way."

Tank mumbled under his breath when he and Josh were assigned the seats farthest back. "I wanted to sit in front with the pilot so I could see better," Tank whispered to Josh.

"We can see just fine from here," Josh replied, shoving aside a newspaper that had been left on his seat.

Mr. Wharton and Mr. Catlett sat directly in front of the boys, while Alicia slid into the seat next to the pilot.

"Everybody set?" Sven asked, his voice raised to be heard above the roar of the piston-powered, single-engine plane. When everyone assured him they were ready, Sven replied, "Then let's go fishing."

Alicia giggled at the remark, making Tank roll his eyes and force a phony giggle that only Josh could hear.

But Josh didn't really notice because his eyes had fallen on the forgotten newspaper. The headlines leaped up at him. Josh snatched up the page and scanned the first paragraph.

Suddenly, Josh knew why Alex and his uncle had disappeared.

Chapter Nine

A DOUBLE SURPRISE

Josh was so excited at his discovery that he wanted to immediately share it with Tank. But it was too noisy in the airplane to talk, so Josh reluctantly folded the newspaper. He put it away until he and Tank could speak privately.

Some of the high ranges over which they flew had strips of snow in low spots near the peaks. The floatplane played tag with low clouds that partially obscured the land below. But when the plane slowed and nosed down, Josh's anxiety rose. There seemed to be nothing but mountains and trees below, and no sign of any place to land.

The June sun, breaking through the overcast, reflected briefly off a small lake fed by several streams. Josh sighed with relief when the plane passed over the final mountain, skimmed low above the treetops, and touched down on the water.

The pilot taxied to a small dock where a husky man ran down a path from the main lodge, a rustic, log structure sitting on a knoll overlooking the lake. A wide front porch ran the length of the building, and there were steps all around the porch but no railings.

Alicia opened her door as the burly man deftly secured the plane to the dock.

"Welcome to Nanook Lodge, everyone," he cried heartily as they disembarked. "You're our first guests of the season. Trent, it's sure good to see you again."

Mr. Wharton, who owned this lodge and many others like it, replied, "You too, Henry." Turning to the others, Alicia's father said, "This is Henry Harper, our friendly lodge keeper. He'll show you to your quarters, but first, say good-bye to our pilot. He'll be back in two days, if the weather permits."

I hope Dad's with you then, Josh thought wistfully as he waved to Sven Swensen.

As the group walked toward the lodge, Tank nudged Josh and whispered, "Did you notice the silly look on Alicia's face when she said good-bye to Sven?"

Josh merely nodded, his thoughts turning to how soon he and Tank could privately discuss the newspaper story.

Mr. Wharton said, "After Henry shows you to your cabins and you unpack, we should all gather in the dining room to meet our fishing guide and have a little something to eat."

The lodge keeper shook his head as he gathered up Alicia's bags. "I unexpectedly had to hire a new bull cook, and he's a little slow yet. So I apologize because we won't have any food until noon. Meanwhile, boys, please grab your stuff and follow me."

Tank asked, "Mr. Harper, what's a bull cook?"

Before he could answer, Alicia explained, "He's a cook's

helper who works in camps like these. He makes the salads and breads, washes the dishes, that kind of thing. Or he may also be a handyman, janitor, or whatever is needed."

Following Mr. Harper with their baggage, Josh asked hopefully, "Will we see any bears?"

"You certainly will. In fact, they'll walk by your windows. Just leave them alone and they'll usually do the same for you. The guide will tell you more about that."

"Speaking of bears," Alicia said, turning to look at the boys, "Nanook Lodge takes its name from the Eskimo word for polar bear, although neither Daddy or I know why the builder called it that. Those ice bears are never found this far south or inland."

Tank said under his breath, "She's as bad as Ryan, a real know-it-all."

"Let's get along with her," Josh replied quietly. When Tank muttered, Josh added in a whisper, "I've got something to show you when we're alone."

A row of cabins stood in back of the lodge near a line of spruce trees. Mr. Wharton and his daughter would stay in the one to the left of the cabin shared by Josh, Tank, and Mr. Catlett.

Entering the cabin, Josh saw against the wall in front of him a propane heater, a lamp, washbasin, window, and a can with fire starter for the wood-burning stove in the right-hand corner. To his left, Josh saw twin bunk beds and a bathroom.

Mr. Catlett finished hanging his clothes on a bar between the foot of the beds on the far wall, then said he was going outside to look around.

The moment the boys were alone, Josh pulled out the newspaper. "Look at this," he said excitedly.

Puzzled, Tank glanced at the paper and read aloud. "'Anchorage police today are looking for a suspected New York underworld crime figure who was stopped last night for having one taillight out. He was released after the arresting officer's radio call showed there were no outstanding warrants for the name listed on his driver's license.'"

Tank looked at Josh with questions in his eyes, but Josh impatiently motioned for him to keep reading.

Shrugging but obviously not understanding Josh's concern, Tank resumed reading. "'Later, the arresting officer recalled that he had seen photos of a man wanted on an out-of-state warrant. At police headquarters, the officer compared wanted pictures and determined that the man he had stopped was Louis Vincent.'"

Tank stopped reading. "I don't get it."

"You will!" Josh replied and picked up the story where Tank had left off. "'Vincent allegedly belonged to a New York racketeering ring, whose top boss recently started serving a federal prison sentence for a mob hit as a result of testimony given by an unnamed witness. Vincent skipped bail after being arrested for threatening the witness.'"

Josh glanced up from the paper and saw the light of understanding start to show in his friend's eyes. Josh hurriedly read on. "'Louis Vincent is known to law enforcement officials as Louie the Enforcer.'" Josh looked at Tank with wide eyes. "That day in the woods, I heard Alex mention a Louie. It must be the same one."

"He's the one who was after Alex and his uncle!" Tank said.

"More likely just the uncle," Josh guessed, "but Alex is now in danger because he's with the man who testified against the crook."

"And Louie was closing in on them," Tank said, his voice rising in excitement. "So they disappeared in the middle of the night. Unless Louie got them! Do you think he did?"

"No, I don't. Remember, we saw Louie back at the house looking for them the day after they left."

"So you think Alex and his uncle are still safe?"

"I hope so." Josh tapped the paper. "But this Louie must really be good at finding people. The paper also says the unidentified man who testified against him was placed in the federal witness protection program."

"What's that?"

"I'm not exactly sure, but I've heard about it. The government tries to protect people who testify against violent criminals. The witnesses are given new identities and hidden away where the criminals can't take revenge on them." Josh read aloud the last paragraph in the newspaper. "'Local authorities are now looking for Vincent but were unable to explain why he was in Alaska.'"

"Well, we know why." Tank took a couple of quick paces in the cabin. "But we can't tell the police until the pilot returns in two days. We could tell my dad, though."

"I'm afraid there's not much he could do," Josh said

thoughtfully. "But maybe there's a telephone or radio at the lodge."

"Yeah! Let's find out!"

The boys rushed out of the cabin. Mr. Catlett wasn't in sight as the friends ran toward the lodge.

"What I can't understand," Josh said as they hurried along, "is how Alex got mixed up in this. The paper said that the name of the witness is not known, but he is thought to be a middle-aged bachelor."

"That figures," Tank replied.

The boys ran up the lodge steps and through the large double doors. There was no lobby, so the boys stopped inside on the wood floors. Straight ahead, about a dozen comfortable chairs circled a large, round, rock fire pit and fireplace.

"Nobody here," Tank said.

"Let's try through that door," Josh suggested.

They entered the separate dining area, which had log benches on each side of four long tables. The boys followed the sound of clanking dishes and cooking utensils coming through an open door at the rear of the room.

The back screen door swung shut and footsteps sounded outside as the boys stopped inside the kitchen. Hurrying to catch up, Josh and Tank darted past the eight-burner range, industrial-sized sink, and two huge commercial refrigerators and freezers.

As the spring snapped the back door shut behind them, Josh saw a man in a white uniform and apron moving around in the dimly lit pantry.

"Must be the cook," Josh commented as he approached the small side room. The doorsill showed deep scratch marks where bears had tried to break in to get at the metal containers of flour, sugar, and other dry goods.

"Hi!" Josh called.

Immediately, the man inside whirled about, his hands snapping into a defensive position.

"Sorry!" Josh apologized, taking a quick step back. "I didn't mean to startle you, mister."

For a second, the man stared at the boys, then turned away.

Josh and Tank exchanged puzzled looks, then Josh asked, "Is there a telephone or radio so we can send a message to Anchorage?"

Over his shoulder, the man snapped, "This is a wilderness camp, so all we have is a ham radio, but it's not working."

Walking away in disappointment, Josh commented, "Not very friendly, was he?"

"Well, we scared him half to death," Tank said. "Did you see how he turned around, ready to fight when you spoke to him?"

"Maybe he thought we were bears sneaking up on him."

"Yeah. Bears talk," Tank said with mock sarcasm.

Josh grinned. "Anyway, let's go tell your dad about the newspaper story and see what he suggests."

Being careful to avoid further contact with the cook, the boys retraced their path and ended up back in the main room of the lodge.

"Oh, there you are," Alicia said from where she sat in one of the comfortable chairs by the fireplace. Her father and Mr. Catlett sat between her and a tall, slender man in his twenties. Alicia added, "We thought you got lost."

Tank's dad rose, saying, "Boys, this is Tad Trumble, our fishing guide. Tad, meet my son, Tank, and his friend Josh Ladd."

After shaking hands, Tad said, "I usually wait for other fishermen to arrive to give my orientation and safety talk. But they won't be joining us for a couple more days, so we'll start now and be ready to fish early tomorrow."

"Will we see a bear?" Josh asked, still sorry that he had not seen the one at Tank's house.

Chuckling, Tad assured him, "You'll see plenty of bears, so let's talk about how to behave around them. We've got both black and brown bears, or grizzlies as they're also called," Tad began. "Both kinds are unpredictable. Usually, they will run away if given a chance. However, temperaments differ, so one bear may run away while another will charge. Of course, a sow* with cubs will be very protective, so don't get between her and the cubs."

Tank asked, "Can you outrun a bear?"

Alicia made a strangled sound as though choking at the idea of such a silly question.

Tad grinned. "I don't have to—all I have to do is outrun one of you." He chuckled along with the two fathers, and then his face grew serious. "A bear can outrun a horse, so obviously they can outrun humans. That's why we make noise and let the bears know we're coming. They usually get out of the way. Try to avoid encounters."

"Yes," Alicia agreed. "That's the best way to avoid trouble."

Tank shot Josh a meaningful look as if to say, *She thinks she knows everything*.

Josh just smiled, unwilling to let Alicia get under his skin.

"Bears have a great sense of smell," Tad continued, "but reportedly have poor eyesight. I'm not sure that's true, but a couple of times when I saw a bear before it saw me, I stood still. It didn't catch my scent and apparently didn't see me."

Tad waited to see if there were any questions, and then picked up again. "For such a big animal, a bear can sneak up on a man without being heard. On the other hand, when a 400- to 600-pound bear charges, it makes the ground shake. A bear can kill with one swipe of its paw. So always treat any bear with respect and give it the right-of-way."

The orientation continued for some time so that when Tad finished, bits of bear information darted about in Josh's brain. For the first time, he wasn't quite sure he actually wanted to see a bear in the wild.

"Dad," Tank said as they all stepped out onto the wide porch, "Josh and I need to talk to you."

"Can it wait?" Mr. Catlett asked. "Trent wants Alicia and me to go with him and Tad to plan tomorrow's outing."

Tank glanced at Josh, who nodded at him.

"I guess it can wait," Tank told his father.

Josh suggested they go explore the camp, so he and Tank wandered down to the lake, talking about the newspaper story and wondering about Alex and his uncle.

"Maybe Alex's folks died or got killed," Josh said, trying to put the pieces of the puzzle together. "His uncle would have to be a brother to either Alex's mother or father. If that uncle was Alex's only living relative, then they would have to live together."

"Even if the uncle was in the witness protection program?"

"I suppose it would be that or go live in a foster home or an orphanage." Josh turned away from the lake and headed toward a chest-high line of brush. "Hey, you know what? Maybe Louie found out about that, and he just followed Alex when he went to stay with his uncle."

"Could be. But where are they now?" Tank wondered.

Josh led the way along a path that had been made through the brush. Suddenly, he stopped. "Listen!"

Both boys froze for a moment.

Tank whispered, "What is it?"

Josh whispered back, "I think we're on one of those game trails that Tad mentioned, and there's something coming toward us."

Tank's eyes opened wide. "Must be a bear! Let's get out of here!"

"Make noise," Josh reminded him. He began clapping his hands and shouting the way Tad had taught them. "Hey, bear! Hey, bear!"

Tank did the same, and they both tried not to panic as

they moved through the brush toward the open space that led to the lodge.

A voice called out, "Where? Where's a bear?"

Josh and Tank stopped in surprise. The voice seemed to be coming from the brush ahead of them.

"That's not a bear," Josh said in a low tone. "It's somebody coming through the brush."

"That was a kid's voice, but we're the only ones here besides Alicia—and it sure wasn't her voice."

Josh and Tank stepped out of the brush and into a clearing. They stopped and looked back as someone stepped out of the brush behind them. Both boys stared with shocked expressions on their faces.

"Alex!" they exclaimed together.

Chapter Ten

DANGER AT THE RIVER

For a moment, the three boys stared at each other in total surprise.

Josh recovered first. "Alex, is that really you?"

Instead of answering, Alex asked anxiously, "How did you guys get here?"

"We flew in to do some fishing," Tank explained.

Josh asked, "Why did you disappear in the middle of the night back in Fireweed?"

Alex started to turn away. "I've got to go."

"Hey, wait!" Josh called. "We want to be your friends."

Alex began walking toward a sparse stand of spruce trees on the knoll. He said over his shoulder, "I've got no friends. Now leave me alone!" He broke into a run, passed the trees, and disappeared behind the line of cabins at the back of the lodge property.

Tank asked softly, "What's wrong with him?"

"Judging from that newspaper story, I think maybe he's scared that if we found him, so can that Louis Vincent, who's been following him."

"So he's afraid?"

"More like *terrified*, I think," Josh said. "Remember how his uncle told us to go away when we tried to see Alex? He obviously didn't want anyone getting too close."

"Yeah. So?"

"The man in the pantry at the lodge quickly turned his back on us. We never really got a good look at him, any more than we did Alex's uncle back in Fireweed. But I have a strong feeling that the uncle and the man in the pantry are one and the same."

"You really think so?" Tank said.

Josh nodded. "Remember how the man in the pantry whirled around and brought up his fists to defend himself when we spoke to him? He probably thought Louie had caught up with him."

"If you're right, what are we going to do?"

"I don't know." Then Josh added thoughtfully, "I wish my dad were here."

"Mine is," Tank reminded him.

"Of course! Let's go tell him what's going on."

The boys found Tank's father talking to Henry Harper by the fireplace. Seeing the concern on the boys' faces, Mr. Catlett asked the lodge keeper to excuse him.

Standing on the wide front porch, the boys took turns telling Tank's father about the newspaper story, their encounter with the man in the pantry, and the appearance of Alex.

"So, Dad, what should we do?" Tank asked when they had finished.

"It's true that there's no telephone," Mr. Catlett said thoughtfully, "and awhile ago, Henry told me the radio is broken. They're waiting for a part to come in on the next plane. So we had better start by telling Henry everything. He has a right to know that this Uncle Bill might also be the new bull cook he hired."

They found the lodge keeper inspecting deep scratch marks on a side window of the lodge. "Bears keep trying to break in," he explained, then he noticed how serious Mr. Catlett and the two boys looked. "What's up?" he asked.

Henry listened in silence until the whole story had been told. Then he commented, "You're right about the bull cook. Calls himself Bill York. I don't know if that's his real name or not. He said the boy, Alex, is his sister's son. His parents were both killed in a plane crash last year."

Tank said, "Josh, you figured it out pretty well."

Josh sighed deeply but didn't reply.

The lodge keeper frowned. "I should have guessed something was up when my regular bull cook left so suddenly. That was the same day that some man flew in from Anchorage and talked to him. I don't know who the man was or what he said to my bull cook, but I was left without a cook's helper just before fishing season started."

"Let me guess," Mr. Catlett said. "The next day, this fellow, Bill York, showed up."

"That's right. He said he had learned to cook in Alaska lumber camps but had been Outside for a couple of years. I was desperate, so I hired him. Turned out he's almost as good as the regular cook."

"What should we do now?" Josh asked.

Mr. Catlett suggested, "I think Henry and I should talk this over with Trent Wharton. He has a right to know since he owns this lodge."

With that agreed upon, Josh and Tank drifted toward their cabin, discussing the problem. On the way, they noticed a little shack that was open except for mesh mosquito screens all around it. Through the screens, Josh noticed someone moving.

"That's Alex," Josh said. "Let's go see what he's doing."

"He'll probably run away again."

"Maybe, but it's worth a try."

As they approached, Alex looked up at them from where he had been cleaning a big fish. He dropped his skinning knife and hurriedly began washing his hands.

Tank warned, "He's going to run."

"Please, wait!" Josh called, rushing toward Alex.

The younger boy suddenly yelled, "Stop, you guys!" When Josh and Tank obeyed the sharp command, Alex explained, "Careful of the fence. It's hot."

Neither Josh nor Tank had noticed a couple of wires about three feet off the ground. They were suspended from a post with insulators. Both boys had seen similar electric fences a long time ago at a California dairy.

"Keeps the bears out of this fish-cleaning house," Alex said as Josh and Tank carefully stepped over the fence. "Works off of big batteries."

"We've been wanting to talk to you," Josh said as Alex dried his hands and stepped toward them. "We met before, remember? I'm Josh Ladd. He's Tank Catlett."

"Hi. I'm Alex Wakefield." He glanced toward the lodge. "But I can't talk to you guys."

"We just want to be friends," Josh assured him.

Alex thoughtfully studied them. "You're the same ones who came to our door back in Fireweed, aren't you?"

When Josh and Tank nodded, Alex asked suspiciously, "What're you doing here?"

Josh replied, "My dad's partner owns this lodge, and he invited us here to go fishing with Tank's dad. Mine couldn't come."

A shadow flickered over Alex's eyes.

"I think we know why you're here, Alex," Josh said.

Alex's eyes narrowed in sudden suspicion. "Oh?"

"On the flight in," Josh explained, "I read a newspaper story about a secret witness and a man named Louis Vincent, who's looking for him."

Alex swallowed nervously. "I've got to go."

"Please! Not yet!" Josh impulsively reached out to touch Alex on the shoulder. "We want to help."

"Nobody can help." Glancing around anxiously, Alex blurted, "My uncle said we would be safe here. Even Louie couldn't find us. But now you know everything, and you found us. If you did, so can Louie. Uncle Bill will blame me. He always says I can't do anything right!"

"Sure you can!" Josh declared.

"No I can't!" Alex leaped over the hot-wire fence and ran toward the kitchen in the rear of the lodge.

Josh and Tank stared after him, then went to see Mr.

Catlett. When they had located him, Tank's dad explained that he and the lodge keeper had talked the situation over with Alicia's father.

"We all agree," Mr. Catlett said, "that because we can't communicate with anybody until the next plane arrives, we'll protect the boy and his uncle and ensure their safety. The three of us also privately talked with the uncle. At first, he denied everything, but in time he admitted the truth."

When Tank's father paused, Josh prompted, "And?"

"And the boy and his uncle will leave on the first plane out," Mr. Catlett explained. "The uncle has a federal contact in Anchorage, who will move them to a safe place. In the meantime, nobody else is to know anything about this, and everyone is to act as if nothing unusual is going on. So that means everyone goes fishing after lunch."

As the boys turned to leave the lodge, Alicia walked onto the front porch. "What's going on?" she asked them.

Josh stalled. "What do you mean?"

"Awhile ago, I saw you both talking with Mr. Catlett and the lodge keeper. Then I saw them with my dad talking to the bull cook. So what's up?"

"Did you ask your father?" Josh wanted to know.

"He wouldn't tell me," she admitted reluctantly.

Josh said, "Then we can't say anything either."

"Yeah," Tank agreed.

"I'll find out on my own," Alicia declared and quickly walked away.

Watching her retreat, Tank asked, "Do you think she will?"

"Who's going to tell her?"

"You're right. I guess there's nothing more we can do for now. Let's go check our fishing tackle."

On the way to their cabin, the boys found Alex washing down the counter in the fish-cleaning shack.

The friends approached together. Through the mosquito netting, Josh said, "Hi. It's us again." The two boys opened the door of the shack and walked in.

Alex stopped scrubbing. "I told my uncle what you guys said, and I got in trouble. So don't talk to me."

"We just want to help—" Josh began, but Alex cut him off.

"You know a little from that newspaper story," he said sharply, "but what you don't know is that if Louie finds us and sees you talking to me or Uncle Bill, your lives will be in danger, too!"

Josh hadn't thought of that. Neither had Tank, Josh decided after shooting him a quick look.

"It's going to be all right," Josh told Alex. "Tank's father will figure out what to do—"

Alex broke in fiercely. "You both have fathers. I don't. Mine got killed along with my mom." Alex's voice began to break. "I wish I'd died with them!"

"Don't say that!" Josh said, reaching out to touch the boy's shoulder.

"Well, I mean it!" Alex's voice faltered and his eyes welled up with tears. "My uncle never did anything to anybody! He just happened to see a mob hit, and when he tried to do the right thing by testifying, he ended up having to hide like a criminal!"

The pain-filled words continued to pour out of Alex. "I don't blame him for being mad at me all the time. He never got married or had any kids—says he didn't want any. Then suddenly he's stuck with me, because he's my only living relative. Now I have to hide, too, knowing that sooner or later, Louie will catch us. Sometimes I wish we could get it over with. At least, then I wouldn't hurt anymore."

Impulsively, Josh reached out again to Alex, but he drew back. "Now go away before something happens to you, too!" He turned and ran toward the kitchen.

In their cabin, Josh and Tank talked about their frustrations while getting their fishing tackle ready. A half hour later, they returned to the lodge for lunch.

Even though Alicia eyed them suspiciously, Josh and Tank motioned Mr. Catlett aside on the front porch. They repeated what Alex had told them during their conversation.

Josh finished by saying, "Tank and I were wondering what would happen if this Louie shows up while we're all away fishing?"

"The lodge keeper will look out for him."

"Yeah, Dad," Tank replied, "but wouldn't it be safer if the lodge keeper made Alex go fishing with us?"

"I suspect you boys want time to talk to Alex without interruption," Mr. Catlett said with a knowing smile. "Let me check first with Trent and Henry."

After lunch, Tank's father quietly told the boys that it had been arranged for Alex to join them.

The temperature was still in the mid-60s under overcast skies when Tad guided the small band of people along the lakeshore. Everyone wore long pants, hiking boots, and long-sleeved shirts. Everyone had protected their hands, necks, and faces with bugdope, the local name for mosquito repellent.

Each person carried day packs, poles, and waders. Tad had a .41 magnum pistol in his shoulder holster. He said it was just to fire in hopes the noise would drive a bear away if one came too close.

"If I see a bear," Tad explained, "I'll tell you to all bring in your lines and grab your day packs or whatever gear you have. Make it quick, but don't run. You follow me and let the bear have the river."

The guide promised excellent fishing opportunities in a nearby river that fed the lake. There was plenty of time, Tad assured them, because there would again be about 20 hours of daylight.

Tad reminded everyone that when they got into the heavy brush, they were to sing, talk loudly, or clap and chant "Hey, bear, hey, bear" to let any within hearing range slip away.

Josh and Tank were last in the single-file line of seven led by Tad, with Mr. Catlett, Mr. Wharton, Alicia, and Alex following.

Tank asked in a stage whisper, "Josh, why did she have to come along?"

"That's not important," Josh replied in a low voice. "We've got to find a way to talk to Alex alone."

"How? He acts as if we aren't even here."

As the fishermen rounded a point of land, a white

kayak* came into view 50 feet offshore. The lone occupant, wearing a protective helmet and dry suit, lowered his double-bladed paddle. "Any luck?"

"Just starting out," Tad called back. "You fishing or sight-seeing?"

"Exercising," the kayaker answered. "Paddled over from that other camp." He motioned behind him, raised his paddle, then stopped before plunging it into the water. "That boy have red hair? Looks like it from here."

Tad nodded. "Sure does."

"There was a fellow who flew in late yesterday afternoon to our camp. Said he was looking for a redheaded kid, but we told him we hadn't seen one."

Josh saw Alex's face turn pale.

The kayaker added, "That man also said something about a family emergency back home. Could your boy—?"

"No," Mr. Catlett interrupted. "This young fellow couldn't have a family emergency at home. Thanks anyway."

"Okay." The kayaker began paddling. "Good luck."

The group started to walk again—except for Alex, who stood still and looked at Josh and Tank with wide, frightened eyes.

"You're safe with us," Josh assured him, keeping his voice low so he wouldn't arouse Alicia's or Tad's suspicion. "Your uncle will be okay, too."

"I should go back to be with him."

"No," Josh said firmly. "Nothing's going to happen to him while Mr. Harper's around. And you'll be safer with us. Now, let's go on. We can talk later."

They headed upstream, following a game trail away from the lake and into a quiet wilderness of spruce trees, alder clumps, and heavy undergrowth.

At a fallen log by a stump, Tad stopped and pointed to his right. "See that enormous plant over there?"

"Yeah," Tank replied. "Looks like maple leaves, only these are humongous. They must be two feet across."

Alicia laughed. "Touch them and you'll find out they're not like any leaves you've ever seen. That's devils club."

"We've heard of it," Josh said, recalling Ryan's remarks about the plant's stinging stickers.

"Don't dare touch it," Tad warned. "The stalk or spike can grow up to six feet tall, and everything about it can really hurt you. There are several of them around, so be careful. Now, let's enjoy the fishing."

He led the way to head-high willows growing beside the river, which was about 70 feet wide and sheltered by high mountains on both sides.

Standing on a small sandbar by the stream, Tad raised his voice to be heard over the sound of the rushing water. "Everyone spread out about a hundred feet apart so you won't tangle each other's lines," he said. "Keep in sight because it's hard to hear. If I motion you out of the water, please move promptly but don't panic. Now, good luck, everyone."

Pulling on heavy wool socks, Alicia said to Josh, Tank, and Alex, "I bet I can beat you three at catching my limit first."

Josh and Alex just shrugged, but Tank accepted the

challenge. "You can't beat me."

"We'll see," she declared. "I'm going after a big, fat rainbow trout*." She slipped into waders that buttoned to her belt. Taking her spinning reel with a red-and-white banded spoon for a lure, she entered the clear, swift, cold waters.

Tank, wearing hip boots, splashed in after her. He carried a fly casting pole with an orange-colored fur-and-feather tied lure, a favorite of arctic char*.

Josh was glad when Alex in his waders moved farther upstream than anyone else. Josh fished nearest to Alex, hoping for an opportunity to talk with him. For a while, they stood apart in chilling, knee-deep water, casting into eddies or near bank brush, where rainbow trout might hide.

Except for the river's pleasant sounds, there was only the call of small birds common to Alaska's woods: robins, chickadees*, and juncos*. Josh stripped line with his left hand as his father had taught him long ago. He noticed that Alex also knew how to fly-fish.

Josh flipped his rod tip forward, sailing the bright-green line high in the air, then back over his head, and forward again. With each cast, the stripped line grew longer. When it was long enough to reach the spot Josh had chosen, he let the black, woolly worm lure with its red tail settle to the bottom. In a minute, he had a strike. He reeled in the rainbow, but then released it. *Too small*, he reasoned, washing his hands in the icy stream.

Josh brought the rod back over his head, glad that there

was a light wind blowing off the surrounding mountains. The breeze kept mosquitoes, white socks,* and no-see-ums* away. As he prepared to cast, Josh felt the lure snag behind him.

He turned around and saw the wet fly tangled in the willows, cropped short by moose, along the shore. Josh's toes were already aching from the cold water, even in his insulated boots, so he welcomed an excuse to climb out of the river and onto the sandy shore.

After retrieving his bait, Josh decided to change flies. He sat down on an old log and opened the box of flies his father had given him. *I wish he were here*, Josh thought wistfully, adjusting his baseball cap and debating which fly to use.

He heard a faint shout above the sounds of the river and glanced up to see Alicia proudly showing Tank the large fish she had landed. Tank ignored her and kept on fishing.

Josh's gaze came to rest on Alex. *I want to talk to him*, Josh thought. His fingers fell idle, and he sat still for a couple of minutes, deep in thought. Then he wrinkled his nose at an unpleasant odor. *My hands smell—probably from handling that fish*, he told himself, then frowned. *No, it's more like something at a zoo.*

Realizing the stench came from behind him, Josh started to turn around, then froze. He felt hot breath and a cold, wet nose touch the back of his neck.

Chapter Eleven

TRAPPED BETWEEN TWO ENEMIES

Josh sat as though flash-frozen while his heart beat a frenzied tattoo against his ribs. At the same moment, Josh saw Alex turn in the river and look toward him. The boy's eyes opened wide in surprise and terror.

He pointed, his mouth moving, but Josh couldn't hear what he was saying. Instead, Josh heard a slight *whoof* behind him. Leaping up and whirling around, Josh stared straight into the dark eyes of a black bear!

His sudden movements startled the animal, which pivoted and bounded away, smashing down the willows and crashing through alder clumps and spruce trees.

Josh was still standing, adrenaline surging hotly through him, when the bear disappeared into the brush and Alex sloshed through the water in his waders to reach him.

"You all right?" Alex asked in a shaky voice.

Josh suppressed a shudder and nodded. "I remember Tad telling us that bears could sneak up on a person, but I didn't think it would happen to me."

"You're lucky you scared that one away."

"Thank God it ran." Josh glanced toward the river. Everyone was still fishing, unaware of what had just happened.

"You want me to stay with you for a while?" Alex asked.

"Thanks," Josh said sincerely. "I'd appreciate that."

The boys sat on the sandbar, where they could see the others, and Tad could keep an eye on them. Josh was alert for the bear's possible return, but he focused his attention on Alex. "I wanted to see a bear," Josh ruefully confessed, "but not that close."

When Alex smiled, Josh added, "It's nice to have someone to talk to about this, especially a friend who doesn't tease me about being so frightened."

"I understand, because I've been scared so much."

"About Louie?"

"Him, and losing my dad and mom, and maybe even Uncle Bill. He sure says awful things to me."

"You want to talk about it?"

Alex took a long, slow breath before nodding. "Uncle Bill will be mad at me, but he's always mad anyway, so why not?"

Slowly, while tears misted his eyes, Alex shared his painful story, his voice breaking from time to time. Josh listened without interruption while his heart ached for the tragedies that had crumpled Alex's world.

When Alex had finished, both boys were silent for a moment. Then Alex said he didn't feel like fishing anymore, so he removed his waders.

Josh did the same and then said, "So your uncle was a man who lived alone and shunned people, but one night in the city he was minding his own business, when saw a murder. He identified the killer from a police lineup. Later, he testified against the bad guy because he thought it was the right thing to do."

"That's right." Alex pulled on his hiking boots. "They promised to protect him, giving him a new name and everything. He might have been safe if my parents hadn't died and he hadn't sent for me."

"He didn't have to do that," Josh pointed out, slipping on his hiking boots, "even if he was your only living relative. Seems to me that he cares about you."

"It sure doesn't *sound* like he does."

Josh remembered hearing the uncle yell at Alex, and he had to admit to himself that the boy was right. Finally, Josh asked, "Anyway, you think that when you were taken to your uncle, Louie followed?"

"It makes sense. Now he's nearby. You heard what that kayaker said a while ago. Louie's traced us here in the Alaska wilderness. It's my fault, too! If I'd dyed my hair as Uncle Bill wanted, Louie might not have found us. I can't do anything right!"

Josh said fervently, "I don't believe that. And I don't believe Louie's going to get you or your uncle."

Fighting back tears, Alex seemed to grasp at the possibility of hope. "Why do you think that?"

Josh explained quietly, "Because every person is important, and that's why the Bible says God's eye is on the sparrow*, and you're more valuable than any bird. I believe God will protect you."

Alex didn't answer for a long time, then he said, "I'd like to believe that. I used to go to Sunday school when my dad and mom were alive. But now ... " He looked behind Josh without completing his sentence.

Josh spun around, half expecting to see the black bear returning. Then Josh relaxed. "It's just some fisherman coming through the brush, Alex."

Alex leaped to his feet. "It's Louie! He's seen us!"

Josh glanced toward Tad and the other four people. All were still fishing, their backs to Josh and Alex.

Josh cupped his hands to his mouth and shouted, "Mr. Catlett! Mr. Wharton! Tad! Tank! Alicia! Somebody!"

Nobody heard his cries for help because of the river.

"They can't hear you!" Alex yelled. "Come on! Louie won't let you get away either!"

Josh hesitated, taking another look at the stranger charging through the brush. The man had such a stocky build that he seemed to have no neck. His head appeared to sit on his huge shoulders. His black hat was pulled low over his eyes, which were hidden behind dark glasses.

Josh thought fast and convinced himself that he and Alex should run to the others for help, but Louie had obviously foreseen that possibility. He abruptly veered through the brush, putting himself between his victims and their friends.

"Come on, Josh!" Alex cried, scrambling up the bank and past the willows.

"I'm right behind you!" Josh leaped to his feet and followed Alex into the alder clusters and toward the line of trees beyond. He glanced backward before the river disappeared from view. All those in his group still had their backs turned, concentrating on their fishing.

We have to outrun Louie, Josh thought, sprinting after Alex. *Then we'll circle back to Mr. Catlett, Mr. Wharton, and Tad!*

In a few strides, Josh was right on Alex's heels. They fled through dense undergrowth, especially the alders, which seemed to reach out to stop the boys' fearful flight. In the Lower Forty-Eight, alders are typical trees, but in Alaska, most alders don't have a single trunk. Rather, they form a tangled mass resembling brush two or three feet high. The alder clumps are difficult to get through, and they threatened to trip the boys at every step. Still, the two fled, already gasping for breath.

Josh followed Alex over a small rise, where both boys stopped to look back. Louie was struggling to regain his footing after stumbling over a fallen tree.

"This way!" Alex's words made Josh turn around. "This should take us back to the river."

Josh's gaze swept over a small gully leading back through the trees and brush to the right. "I'm coming!" Josh replied and followed Alex into the steep-sided ravine.

Both boys were perspiring in spite of the cool, overcast weather when they again saw the river ahead.

"Do you see Louie?" Alex puffed.

After risking a brief backward glance, Josh answered, "No. Maybe we lost him."

"Good! Let's follow the river. . . ."

Josh didn't hear the rest because the boot on his right

foot caught on an alder clump, and he fell hard. He yelped in pain and sat up fast, clutching his ankle.

"What's the matter?" Alex panted, turning back and quickly kneeling beside Josh.

"I twisted my ankle." Josh tried not to show any sign of the sharp pain he felt.

"Can you walk?"

"I don't know." Josh struggled to his feet, then almost fell.

"Here," Alex instructed. "Lean on me. We've got to get out of sight before Louie finds us again."

Wincing in agony, Josh struggled to stand. With great determination and Alex's help, he was able to reach a growth of willows along the riverbank. The boys crawled into the grove, then sprawled on their stomachs while the pain in Josh's right leg rapidly grew worse.

For half a minute, they lay in silence, listening hard. The only sound was the distinctive, rapid chickadee call in the woods. The boys' eyes probed the area behind them.

Finally, with a sigh, Josh whispered, "I think we lost him."

"You don't know Louie," Alex warned. "He'll be back on us before you know it."

Josh was afraid that was true. He shifted his attention to the river. It seemed to be much deeper water because it was swifter, darker, and quieter than where they had been fishing.

"Maybe we can slip down to the bank," Josh said, "and work our way back to the others. If we stay out of Louie's sight ... Listen!"

"What?"

"Shhh!"

Above the sound of the river, they heard another noise—a deep, threatening growl.

"Bear!" Alex whispered. "But where?"

"There!" Josh pointed. "But it's not that same black one. That's a grizzly!"

Both boys fell into awed, frightened silence as an immense boar* bear emerged from the brush on the far side of the river. It charged into the shallows by a gravel bar and slapped at the water, making the massive hump on its great shoulders quiver.

"He's in a bad mood," Josh whispered.

"Real bad," Alex agreed. "And he's the biggest bear I've ever seen in my life!"

Suddenly, the grizzly stopped and stood upright on its hind legs, sniffing noisily. It seemed to be at least 10 feet tall. Then it let out a thunderous growl and clicked its long teeth menacingly while swinging its broad head from side to side.

Alex whispered, "I think he's got our scent."

The bear dropped to all four feet and circled the gravel bar, sniffing and letting out a deep rumble from its shaggy chest. "The wind must be shifting because of the mountains," Josh hoarsely whispered back. "He can't be sure where we are."

"We're caught between that bear and Louie."

The pain in Josh's ankle reminded him of another

problem. If he couldn't be given some kind of first aid soon, he might not be able to walk. He knew a doctor would be needed as quickly as possible.

"We can't stay here," he said in a low voice. "And we can't go back because of Louie, so we've got to get by that bear to reach Tank and the others."

"How are we going to do that?" Alex demanded, almost forgetting to keep his voice down. "No matter which way we go, we're in terrible danger!"

Josh silently admitted Alex was right as he watched two mergansers* fly past and land in the river. Instantly, the bear charged the ducks. They took off again, making the bear slap the water in frustration.

"Can't go that way," Josh said.

"Can't stay here either," Alex replied. "Louie will catch us before we know it."

The bear crawled out on the gravel bar and shook itself, spraying water everywhere like a dog that's just been bathed. Suddenly, it stopped and again sniffed the air.

"I think he's got our scent again," Alex whispered.

"Or maybe Louie's." Josh turned to look back. "I see somebody moving just beyond those trees!"

Alex groaned in despair. "Louie! If he sees us . . . "

"Shhh! Stay still and hope . . . Wait!" Josh lifted his head. "That's not Louie! That's Tank!" Then he whispered in sudden alarm. "He's going to walk right into . . . Alex! What're you doing?"

The redheaded boy crawled out of the willows. "Going to warn him!"

Josh started to sit up, but the movement caused a stab of sharp pain in his ankle. He grabbed it in a useless effort to ease the agony.

Alex had gotten to his feet. He bent over and ran toward Tank, who was slowly making his way through the brush and trees. With a quick, desperate prayer, Josh turned to look at the bear. It stood on the gravel bar, sniffing the air.

He must have lost the scent again, Josh told himself with relief. *I just hope it's true that bears don't have very good eyesight.* Josh was also glad that the bear was below, making it harder for the bear to see him.

Josh twisted his head to watch Alex leading Tank to the edge of the brush, where they dropped to their knees and crawled into the willows with Josh.

Tank whispered, "Where's that bear?"

"There!" Alex pointed.

All three boys peered through the willows as the grizzly slapped at a piece of driftwood floating by.

Tank said hoarsely, "Wow! He's a monster!"

"A very mad monster," Alex amended.

"Maybe he's been shot or wounded," Josh said. "Or maybe he's got a sore jaw or something."

"Or maybe," Tank suggested, "he's simply bad-tempered, like some people."

Then Josh asked him, "What're you doing here?"

"I could ask you guys the same thing," Tank replied. "I looked up from fishing just as you two ran into the trees. I waited, but when you didn't come back, I changed to my boots and followed, but I lost you."

"You didn't see a man chasing us?" Josh asked.

"What man?"

"Louie!" Alex whispered. "He's lost us for a while, but he'll find us."

Tank exclaimed, "Then let's get out of here."

"We can't," Alex explained. "The bear's between us and our group, and Josh twisted his ankle."

For the first time, Tank noticed the pained look on Josh's face. Tank asked anxiously, "How bad is it, Josh?"

"I don't know, but it sure hurts."

"Can you walk on it?" Tank asked.

"I don't think so." He unlaced his right boot, gingerly removed his sock, then sucked in his breath at what he saw. The ankle had swollen to the size of a grapefruit and was already turning an ugly reddish-purple color.

Alex exclaimed, "Looks like a sprain the way it's swelled up. I had a sprain once. You'll be on crutches for a while."

Josh ruefully admitted, "I think it's going to need more than just simple first aid."

"The nearest doctor is in Anchorage," Tank said. "But you can only get there when Sven returns with his plane."

The grizzly's angry roar caused all three boys to turn in its direction. The huge bear stood on its hind legs again, sniffing and clicking its terrible teeth. After a moment, it dropped to all four legs, left the gravel bar, and scrambled up the far bank before again testing the air.

Josh explained, "The wind keeps changing, so he can't

keep our scent and know for sure where we are."

"Yeah," Tank murmured, "if he ever does, he'll come straight for us."

"If Louie doesn't find us first, that is," Alex replied.

All three boys glanced anxiously behind them, but there was no sign of their pursuer.

Josh commented, "Alex, it was very brave of you to warn Tank a few minutes ago."

"It wasn't bravery," Alex protested. "It had to be done, and your ankle wouldn't let you do it."

Tank replied, "Well, you kept me from blundering into that grizzly or maybe Louie. Thanks."

Josh's pain was increasing so much that it was hard to think about anything else. However, he tried to get his mind off of it. "Alex," he began, "surely Louie wouldn't hurt all three of us if he finds us."

"You don't know Louie. Uncle Bill told me some of the crimes Louie's committed. Lives mean nothing to him." Alex hesitated, then said, "I don't wish anybody bad luck, but I do wish that bear would chase him away."

"Can't count on that," Josh observed. "So we've got to get ourselves out of this mess, and soon."

Alex said, "The only way to safety is to slip past that bear and get back to Tad and the others."

Tank snorted. "Oh, sure! Just slip by a mad grizzly with Josh's bum leg ... while trying to avoid Louie." He paused for a moment, then continued, "My dad and the others must be looking for us by now. We can just wait for them."

As Josh pondered Tank's suggestion, he heard the

sound of an airplane and looked up. "That's Sven's float-plane," Josh whispered. "He's come back early."

"Yeah," Alex replied somberly. "Tank, I don't like to dis-agree with you about Josh, but we've got to get him back to the lodge before Sven takes off again. If we don't, it'll be at least another 24 hours before Josh can get to a doctor. By then, that ankle will be in terrible shape." To Josh he said, "You'll be hurting a lot more than you are now."

Josh's pain made him agree. "You're probably right. So we've all got to slip by that bear. We'll have to crawl through the brush along this side of the shore and head back to find the others so they can help me back to camp."

"You're pupule!" Tank exclaimed, lapsing into use of the common Hawaiian word for *crazy*.

"There's no other way," Josh insisted.

"But that's too risky!" Tank protested.

"Sure, it's risky," Alex admitted, "but we can't stay here. That bear might finally get our scent and come straight over here—if Louie doesn't find us first. We're also running out of time because we've got to get help before that plane takes off without Josh."

After hesitating, Josh nodded. "Let's go." He started crawling through the willows and instantly grabbed his ankle. "I can't make it. You two go on without me," he urged.

"No," Alex replied. "Tank, you stay with him. I'll go get help."

Before Josh or Tank could object, Alex slid away through the willows.

Chapter Twelve

HURT, HELPLESS, AND ALONE

Watching Alex slip purposefully away, Josh whispered to Tank, "He says he can't do anything right, but look at him!"

"Yeah, he's sure trying. But can he really make it by himself?"

"He'll have to," Josh said. "He's too far away to call back without either the bear or Louie hearing us."

"Maybe I can catch up with him."

"What?"

Tank didn't explain, but asked, "Can you stay here by yourself for a while?"

"Well, I guess so, but—"

"We've got a better chance of getting out of this mess if Alex and I can get help," Tank interrupted. "And I think we have a better chance of finding the others if we work together. I know it's a risk, but I'm going with Alex."

"Louie's more likely to see the two of you running than just Alex by himself."

"Yeah, but if he chases us, we're more likely to lose him

than you are. Besides, I can't let Alex do that alone. So you stay out of sight, and we'll bring back my father, Mr. Wharton, and Tad as fast as we can."

Before Josh could protest, Tank crept through the willows after Alex.

Josh winced from the pain in his ankle and tried to shut out the terrible possibilities of what could happen to Tank and Alex. *Or to me*, he thought.

He carefully looked around. Already, Tank and Alex were out of sight somewhere in the riverbank brush. To the right, back of the alders and spruce, there was no sign of Louie either. Only the bear was visible to Josh's left, across the river. The animal bounded up and down the small gravel bar, still in a foul mood. Suddenly, it plunged into the river and started swimming across.

Oh, Lord, no! The bear will get Tank and Alex for sure!

Terrified and helpless, Josh watched the swift water begin to sweep the bear downstream.

Josh held his breath until the mighty grizzly got about a third of the way across. Then, abruptly, it turned and swam back to the gravel bar.

Josh's chest trembled with a sigh of relief. Then he glanced back toward the trees to his right and swallowed hard. He heard a rustling not far away and told himself frantically, *It's Louie—he's coming this way!*

Fighting against the excruciating pain in his ankle, Josh grabbed his boot in one hand and crawled quietly down to the riverbank, clenching his teeth to avoid crying out in anguish. He stopped at the water's edge. He couldn't see

Louie from his new hiding place.

From 50 yards away, Josh saw that Tank and Alex had left the sheltering brush. He watched as they dropped down from the top of the riverbank onto a long, narrow strand of sand. High water had eroded the soil so the top of the bank was only about eight feet above the sand.

There, motionless but in plain sight, the two boys crouched against the steep side of the riverbank. A couple of feet to their left, the swift-running stream surged by.

They're afraid the bear will see them if they move, Josh realized. *It probably can't hear them over the noise of the river, but that doesn't mean it can't smell them.*

Josh's gaze switched back to bear, which again was testing the air with its keen nose. Then it bounced off the gravel bar, up the bank, and disappeared into the brush on the opposite side of the river.

Maybe it's leaving for good, Josh hopefully thought. *Now if Louie will just do the same. . . .*

Looking up behind him, Josh glimpsed Louie standing motionless about 25 feet away. For about a minute, he remained still, looking toward the opposite shore. Apparently, he, too, had seen the bear bound off into the brush.

From his angle, Louie could not see Tank and Alex. Then, seeming satisfied that the grizzly wasn't coming back, Louie began cautiously making his way along the bank. He searched the willows, looking for the boys.

If he looks down or comes much closer, he'll see me! Josh realized. *I can stay here and hope he doesn't see me. If he passes by and goes down the bank far enough, maybe I can crawl to the alders and underbrush to hide. If the bear doesn't come back, I could cross the river.*

Josh carefully reached out and eased a finger into the water. *No! It's too cold—probably less than 40 degrees. I'll die of hypothermia.* Then he remembered the bear's unsuccessful effort to cross the fast-flowing stream, and he added, *Or I would drown.*

Quickly scanning the area, Josh saw that there wasn't a log or anything on which he might drift downstream to safety. Shaking his head, Josh recognized he couldn't use the river to escape, even if the bear didn't return.

That leaves only two possibilities, he told himself. *Either Louie doesn't find me and I stay hidden here until Tank and Alex bring help, or I can try to crawl inland and circle back the way we came. But that will be nearly impossible with this swollen ankle.*

Silently debating with himself, he swung his gaze back to Tank and Alex. Motionless, they watched to see if the grizzly would return. They were still below Louie's line of sight, so he couldn't see them.

They're not making any progress, Josh realized. *Not that I blame them. But if Louie comes down closer to the water, he'll be able to see both them and me.*

His ankle was hurting so much that he pulled up his pant leg and gulped. *It looks even bigger*, he thought with rising concern. *It's still swelling up.*

Gazing at the still-cloudy sky, Josh warned himself, *Sven might fly away before we get back, and if he does . . .* Josh shook off a sudden fear of what might happen to his ankle if he didn't receive treatment soon. *I've got to do something, but what?*

Time passed with agonizing slowness as Josh lay huddled in the willows, silently praying for guidance. He heard his relentless pursuer drawing closer, shoving the willows aside.

Suddenly, the bear roared from somewhere upstream. Josh heard Louie rustling in the brush and assumed he was watching the bear. In spite of his precarious situation, Josh raised his head to peer through the thin branches.

Less than 20 feet away, Louie stood with his back to Josh, watching the grizzly. It had reappeared on the opposite shore about 200 yards beyond where Tank and Alex still crouched, motionless.

Again, the grizzly stood on its hind legs, tested the air, bellowed angrily, and leaped into the water.

Josh's mind warned, *It's got the scent again!*

In helpless silence, Josh watched the bear stroking powerfully toward the center of the stream. This time, it did not turn back. It swam straight across and bounded out of the water 100 yards beyond where Tank and Alex were still hunched over. Their backs were to the bear as it violently shook water from its fur before bounding through the willows and up onto the top of the riverbank.

Oh, no! If it comes this way—Josh's thought snapped off as the bear slowly walked along the edge of the bank. *Here it comes!*

In horror, Josh realized the huge creature was going to pass right above where Tank and Alex were crouched on the sand. Jerking his attention from that terrible sight, Josh shot a glance toward Louie. *He's gone!*

Josh raised his head higher and scanned the area. *Is Louie giving up?* Josh asked himself. *Is he just trying to slip around to intercept Tank and Alex? No, most likely he decided to go back into the woods while the bear was in the water. But where is he now?*

Swinging his attention back to the boys, Josh jerked in alarm. *What are they doing? No!* his mind silently screamed. *Tank! Alex! Stop! Don't do that!*

***

Below the bank, unaware that the bear was approaching them, Alex leaned over to Tank and whispered, "I don't hear it anymore. Maybe it gave up."

"I sure hope so."

"Well, Louie won't. You can be sure of that. If we don't get word to Sven before he takes off again, Josh could have real trouble with that ankle. We've got to get to your dad, Mr. Wharton, and Tad—"

"Yeah!" Tank interrupted. "Tad's got a gun."

"A handgun probably won't stop a grizzly, but the noise might scare it off," Alex said. "Anyway, we've got to get back to them real fast, and before Louie catches Josh or us."

"Maybe my dad and the others are already looking for us."

"They probably are, but it's not easy trailing us, the way we ran through those trees and brush. We can't wait any longer."

Tank said, "What if that bear isn't gone, and we run into it?"

"Then we'll just have to do the best we can. We're running

out of time. Unless you've got a better idea, let's go."

Tank nodded slowly.

Barely breathing, with Tank right behind him, Alex bent over, hugged the side of the bank and tiptoed along the sandy strand. He was grateful that he could not even hear his own footsteps because of the rushing river.

***

No! No! The silent, distressed words formed in Josh's mind as he watched the bear shuffling along the top of the bank while the two boys unknowingly tiptoed toward it. The grizzly swung its head back and forth, giving Josh a chance to see that the flaring nostrils looked like the lids of five-gallon cans.

Josh realized that neither the boys nor the grizzly could see or hear each other, but the bear could smell them if the fickle wind blew toward it.

Josh kept trying to swallow a lump that had formed in his throat. He found it hard to breathe as he watched the boys and the bear slowly come closer together, still out of each other's view.

The bear repeatedly tested the air but did not stop moving. Ponderously, it shuffled forward. Its humped shoulders moved in such a menacing way that Josh could just imagine the powerful forearms reaching out and smashing out a life in a single blow. Yet Josh was powerless to help.

Holding his breath, he observed the bear slowly closing the gap between itself and the boys.

Josh wasn't a nail-biter, but his hand flew to his mouth as he foresaw what was going to happen. *It's going to pass directly over them! They'll only be about three feet apart! If it gets their scent or hears them* . . .

***

With his right shoulder as close to the wall of the carved-out bank as he could get, Alex crept forward, bent almost double in an effort to make himself as small as possible.

He felt alone and defenseless, although Tank was only a step behind. Neither boy had a weapon. They knew they couldn't outrun the bear if it chased them. It could plunge into the icy water and swim without fear, but a human being would quickly drown or die of hypothermia.

Desperately, Alex sought for something to give him hope, anything to keep him from yielding to the panic that tried to seize control of him.

You are of more value than many sparrows. The words leaped to Alex's mind. *Isn't that what Josh—?*

Alex didn't finish the thought because two small sticks fell from overhead and landed at his feet. He stopped so suddenly that Tank bumped into him. Alex laid a forefinger across his lips, then pointed upward before cupping his ear to listen.

Both boys looked up to the top of the bank barely three feet over their heads. Little bits of dirt, dislodged by huge paws, slid down. Then a growl came, low and mean, from directly overhead.

The boys looked at each other with pure terror on their

faces as the shifting breeze caressed their cheeks and then the back of their necks. They knew the fickle wind currents could easily betray their presence to the bear trying to find them.

Alex thrust his right forefinger into his mouth and held it up, trying to get a better idea of the wind's direction. With relief, he felt his finger cool fastest on the side nearest the bank.

The wind's blowing toward us, he thought. *No! It's changing upstream.*

It was still eddying from different directions. Alex thought wildly, *If it swings to the left and blows across the river toward us, it'll carry our scent up to the bear.*

An angry roar directly overhead told Alex that the bear had caught their scent. It instantly went berserk. Thundering its fury, the bear leaped off the bank and sailed over the boys' heads like a giant truck. Several hundred pounds of dark-brown fur landed in the water with a mighty splash just beyond two terror-stricken boys.

***

Josh's terrified fascination at the drama unfolding in front of him was interrupted by a movement to his right. Out of the corner of his eye, he caught sight of Louie. He had silently moved to stand on top of the bank not 10 feet in front of Josh. Louie stared intently at where the grizzly was just surfacing in the river after its dive.

Louie will find me for sure when he turns around, Josh thought.

For a moment, Josh hesitated, torn by a desire to watch

the bear and the boys. Then, with a fervent silent prayer for Tank's and Alex's safety, Josh gritted his teeth against the pain in his ankle. Clutching his boot close to his chest with one hand, he used the other to help him begin crawling up the bank to the willows behind Louie.

Holding his breath and fighting the pain, Josh quietly eased past the man. *Please don't let him turn around now!* Josh wiggled into the heavy underbrush.

The effort of crawling and the terrible torment in his leg forced Josh to stop behind the first alder clump. Flat on his stomach, he listened. Had Louie seen him? What was the bear doing? Were Tank and Alex safe?

Josh cautiously raised his head to peek through the tangled alder trunks.

Louie had dropped to a crouch, obviously trying to keep the grizzly from spotting him. Josh flashed a look toward the river but couldn't see or hear the bear.

There was a terrible silence broken only by a chickadee's repetitious calls.

Suddenly, Louie turned and looked directly at Josh. With a sadistic smile, Louie slowly straightened up.

"There you are!" he said and rushed toward the boy.

Josh forced himself to his feet but couldn't put any weight on his ankle. In spite of excruciating pain, he started hobbling on one foot as fast as possible through the tangled undergrowth.

Louie's triumphant laugh mocked Josh's flight.

I can't outrun him, he thought. *He's going to get me unless I can think of something fast!*

Chapter Thirteen

OUT OF CHOICES

Tank and Alex stood frozen against the bank as the grizzly turned in the water, lifted its massive head, and sniffed while paddling to keep from being swept downstream. Then it bellowed and began swimming directly toward the two boys.

"Run!" Alex screeched, shoving himself away from the bank and sprinting along the sand. "Run! Run!"

"I am! I am!" Tank cried, almost stepping on the other boy's flying heels.

Alex risked a quick glance over his shoulder at the bear. "He's gaining on us!"

"Oh, Lord! Help us!" Tank's prayer was a moan.

The steep bank beside them curved to the left, completely blocking off the sandy strand on which they were running. Alex didn't dare chance another look back for fear of tripping and falling. Instead, his eyes probed ahead, desperately seeking some way to escape the terrible fate rapidly overtaking him.

A panicked sob escaped his mouth at what he saw. "The

bank ahead is too steep to climb! We're going to be trapped!"

***

Josh forced himself to keep moving, carrying his boot, and desperately scrambling away from Louie. In the distance, Josh faintly heard the grizzly's ominous bellow. It seemed to echo through the woods as an almost continuous sound of fury. With a shudder, Josh realized, *That means the bear has seen Tank and Alex!*

Louie slowed to a walk and mockingly called, "Hey, kid, what's your big hurry?"

Josh didn't answer or look around. Hobbling on one foot and trying to keep the injured one from bumping into the brush, Josh tripped on an exposed tree root.

"Oh!" The involuntary cry escaped his lips as he fell beside a fallen log and white-hot pain seared his ankle.

"Stay down, boy," Louie urged. "You can't escape."

The wind was knocked out of Josh, and he was aware that his hands were cut and scraped from trying to break his fall. *Got to get up*, he urged himself. *Keep going!* To help himself stand, he reached down with his right arm and closed his fingers around a broken limb about four feet long.

He gripped the limb and used it to shove himself to a sitting position, for the moment forgetting the agony. Using the limb as a cane, Josh managed to regain his footing. He hobbled around the end of the fallen log and was relieved to see a game path through the underbrush. He turned left onto it because it offered easier going.

From a short distance away, Louie sneered and called,

"It's no use, boy. So give it up."

A quick glance back showed Josh that Louie was leisurely following. In his right hand, he held a weapon that Josh hadn't seen before.

Louie apparently saw Josh's eyes shift to the weapon, for he asked, "You never seen a blackjack before, boy? Or maybe you've heard it called a sap. Same thing." He gave Josh a menacing grin and said, "It's a sort of leather club with lead inside. Gives a person a terrible headache, but you won't mind because you're going into the river anyway."

"You'd better leave me alone," Josh puffed, glad that he could see the trail, although waist-high brush clutched at him from both sides. "My friends will be along in a minute."

"I saw your friends." Louie's voice was confident and calm. "Two kids about your age with a mad grizzly after them. It'll save me the trouble of dealing with them. Now, stand still and let's get this over with."

Josh didn't answer but continued his awkward, stumbling effort to escape.

Louie's voice changed. "You're making me mad!"

Josh hitched along as fast as possible with his painful ankle and makeshift cane. Then, ahead, he saw a small clearing with no brush and no alder clumps. *I won't have a chance there*, Josh warned himself furiously. *He'll catch me for sure!*

***

Alex didn't slow his frantic run as he repeated to Tank, "We're trapped!"

"I see that," Tank puffed from behind Alex.

Behind them, the charging bear was closing fast, and the ground seemed to tremble under its weight and speed.

Alex looked up at the bank that had cut off their escape. "It's only about eight feet up to the top, but it's too high to jump," Alex said in a trembling voice. "But we've got to find a way up—fast!"

Frantically glancing about, Alex spotted some tree roots sticking out of the bank. He slowed enough to leap high, wildly grabbing for a root with his right hand. The root was rough, but it held. Alex pulled himself up while reaching for the next root with his left hand.

He grasped it and let go of the first root so Tank could grab it. Alex thought he heard voices just as his full weight pulled on the second root.

It snapped off with a dull, popping sound, dropping Alex on top of Tank. They landed together on the sand. The grizzly closed in on them from 60 feet away.

Slightly dazed by the fall, Alex thought he heard a shout, followed by a gunshot. Shaking his head and trying to disentangle himself from Tank's arms and legs, Alex whirled toward the bear. It was still coming when a second shot cut through the air.

As through a haze, Alex watched the bear slide to a full stop in the sand. Then Alex looked up at the top of the embankment. Several people stood there, waving their arms and shouting loudly.

Quickly squeezing his eyes together and then opening them wide, Alex's vision cleared. As in a dream, he saw Tad aiming his heavy pistol toward the bear. It stood still, slowly moving its head from side to side.

Tank looked up and scrambled to his feet, still panting from the chase. "Dad!" he shouted. "And Mr. Ladd!"

Alex's eyes scanned the others. Alicia and her father, both looking petrified with fear, and—

"Uncle Bill!" Alex shrieked in total surprise.

Tank grabbed Alex's arm. "The bear! Look!"

Alex swiveled his head as the grizzly gave a low *whoofing* sound, then spun around. It ran down the sandy patch, plunged into the water, and paddled rapidly toward the opposite shore.

Alex's uncle and Alicia's father reached down from the top of the riverbank. Each grabbed one of Alex's arms and pulled him up while Tad, Mr. Catlett, and Josh's father did the same with Tank.

When Alex's feet touched the top of the embankment where the others stood, his uncle impulsively reached out and pulled the boy to his chest. "Oh, Alex! Alex!" he whispered hoarsely, hugging his nephew tightly.

Still breathing heavily, the boy stiffened in surprise. Then he relaxed, crying, "Oh, Uncle Bill!"

Mr. Ladd demanded anxiously, "Where's Josh?"

From the shelter of his own father's arms, Tank pointed downstream. "Back there! His ankle is badly hurt, and Louie's after him!"

Without a word, Mr. Ladd dashed down the bank.

***

With his makeshift cane, Josh hobbled along the game trail through the underbrush that snagged his clothes and slowed his speed. His eyes scanned the open space ahead. *Can't go there*, he warned himself. *Louie will catch me in a second*. Frantically, Josh looked around, desperately seeking some other way to escape.

The explosive sound of a shot startled Josh. He glanced back, thinking Louie was firing a gun at him. Then Josh saw that his pursuer had stopped to look over his shoulder.

Josh heard shouting and another shot. "Those are my friends!" he yelled to Louie. With soaring hopes, Josh added, "They're coming for me, and one has got a gun!"

Louie faced the boy again. "They're too far away to help you." He slapped the blackjack in his open left palm. "I'll take care of you now," he said coldly, starting toward Josh again, "and catch up with those others later."

Josh spun about and stumbled when his injured leg almost collapsed under him. With a mighty effort, he regained his balance and continued hobbling through the brush as fast as possible.

That must have been Tad's gun I heard, Josh told himself. *So Mr. Catlett and the others must have done the shouting. But Louie's probably right. They can't get here in time unless I can stall Louie. But how?*

His searching eyes flashed across something to his right. *Wait!* He took a quick, closer look. A spruce tree had fallen, snapping off so that the stump stood about two feet high. In front of the log, Josh glimpsed broad, maple-shaped green leaves.

Josh felt a surge of hope. *That might work*. He suddenly veered off the game trail.

"Hey! Where are you going?" Louie demanded harshly from behind the fleeing boy.

Josh didn't answer but kept limping along, his mind engrossed in a quickly forming plan. *Got to make Louie change directions*, Josh thought, abruptly swerving to the left. *But this is going to take me closer to him.*

"Now where do you think you're going?" Louie demanded. "Stalling won't help!"

Josh's cane snagged on alder clumps, threatening to throw him facedown into the brush, but somehow Josh kept his footing. He circled in front of the log so Louie also had to change directions.

Josh's lungs were starting to burn from breathing so hard and fast. He drove himself forward, focusing on his objective. *A few more feet.* . . .

"That does it!" Louie shouted. "I'm tired of fooling with you." He broke into a run, heading straight for Josh.

It took all of Josh's willpower to stand still, panting loudly and bracing himself with the cane as Louie rapidly closed the distance between them.

Josh waited, faintly hearing the river in the distance, a chickadee's call, and far-off voices. Josh turned his full attention to Louie, who was rushing toward him.

He was within 10 feet of the fallen log when Josh suddenly changed his mind. *I can't do this!* His thought was instantly followed by a shout. "Stop right there!"

Louie laughed mockingly. "You going to stop me?"

Holding his boot in one hand, Josh threw up his other. "Stop! Please, stop!"

"Sure," Louie answered, leaping over the log.

He landed on his feet, brushing against the huge plant as Josh had planned.

Instantly, Louie shrieked with pain, dropped his weapon, and tried to spin away from the plant. Instead, he tripped and fell across it. His scream became one long, continuous sound as he rolled free of the devils club plant and thrashed about in the underbrush.

Josh started to hobble forward to help the stricken man just as the rescuers rushed into view.

"Dad!" Josh yelled in tremendous relief.

***

Back at the lodge, Tank, Alex, and Alicia stood at the foot of Josh's bed, where he rested after his ankle had been tended. Soon he would be flown to Anchorage to be treated by a doctor.

Josh asked, "How's Louie?"

"Still hurting," Alicia replied, "although Tad used his tweezers to get out the last of all those devils club stinging stickers."

"I'm sorry that happened," Josh admitted, "but I didn't see any other way to stop him."

Alex said grimly, "It serves him right. Uncle Bill says that when the doctor in Anchorage finishes treating Louie, he'll go to prison for a long time."

"Yeah," Tank replied, "then you and your uncle won't have to run and hide anymore."

The door opened and Josh's father entered, followed by Mr. Catlett.

"You ready for Sven to fly us back to Anchorage?" Mr. Ladd asked his son.

"I'm ready." Josh hesitated, then added, "Dad, I can't tell you how much it meant for me to see you back there in the woods."

Mr. Ladd sighed heavily. "Son, I'm sure glad I decided that being with you was more important than any job. I'm also glad I had Sven fly me here early."

Alex said, "Uncle Bill said you landed right after a kayaker stopped at the lodge and mentioned that a man at the next camp had asked about a redheaded kid. Uncle Bill knew what that meant and started out to find me."

"That's right," Mr. Ladd added. "And I went with him."

Tank's father explained, "When I realized all three of you boys were gone, Tad and the rest of us quit fishing and went looking for you."

"We couldn't follow your trail," Alicia explained. "We didn't know what had happened, but when we ran into Mr. Ladd and Alex's uncle, we found out about Louie."

"We might not have found you boys in time," Mr. Ladd said, "if it hadn't been for that bear. Tad guessed that the grizzly had you boys cornered, so we followed its roars."

"Good thing we did, too," Alicia said somberly. "Otherwise, the grizzly—"

"Don't say it!" Tank interrupted.

"Or that terrible man—" Alicia continued.

"Enough, already!" Tank said with a shudder.

"Alex, you once said that you couldn't do anything right," Josh reminded him. "But you sure proved that isn't true this afternoon. You can do *a lot* right."

"Only because of something you said, Josh," the boy said. "I heard a chickadee calling in the bush and thought of what you told me about sparrows. You said God's eye is on the sparrow and His eye is on me, too. I figured if that was right, then Tank and I should be helped to escape from bad old Louie. So I did what I could."

Tank observed, "Alex, when you and I were pulled up that bank to safety, I noticed that your uncle hugged you."

For a moment, Alex didn't answer. He pressed his lips together and blinked rapidly as though fighting back tears. "Sure surprised me. On the way back to the lodge, he admitted that at first he resented me coming to live with him. But after what happened today, he said he realized we need each other. I agree."

Tank turned to Josh. "This all started because you wanted to see a bear. Remember?"

Josh chuckled. "I sure do."

Alicia teased, "You want to see another one?"

"No, thanks," Josh said cheerfully. "I've seen enough bears to satisfy me for a long time."

Mr. Ladd and Mr. Catlett laughed.

"Well, Josh," Tank replied with a grin, "we had a really exciting adventure to start off living here in Alaska. I wonder what our next one will be?"

"Get me on Sven's plane for home," Josh replied, "and then we'll probably find out."

GLOSSARY

CHAPTER 1

Anchorage (ANK-er-age): Originally, steamships used to anchor offshore where a tent city of railroad workers started what is now Alaska's largest city. About half of the forty-ninth state's entire population lives here.

Lanai (LAH-nye): Hawaiian for *patio, porch,* or *balcony.* Also, when capitalized, Lanai is a smaller Hawaiian island.

Sourdough (Sou'r doe): Originally, a yeasty, long-lived concoction early Alaskan pioneers and prospectors used to leaven bread and other baked goods. Now it more commonly means an old-time Alaska resident, especially a Bush resident.

Fireweed: In this story, it's a fictitious Alaskan community. In reality, fireweed is a plant that grows up to six feet tall and has bright-pink blossoms. In late June, blooming begins on the lower stems and the plant gradually blossoms all the way to the top by August or September. When fireweed "tops out," winter is close. Fireweed takes its name from deep horizontal roots that allow fast regrowth after a fire.

Chugiak (CHEW-gee-ak): The middle syllable is like the last syllable in McGee; it's *not* pronounced G or jee. Chugiak, in south-central Alaska, is the gateway to Chugach (CHEW-gatch) State Park, consisting of a half-million acres of pristine wilderness filled with wildlife.

Honolulu (hoe-no-LOO-LOO): Hawaii's capital and the most populous city in the fiftieth state is located on the island of Oahu (oh-WHA-hoo). In Hawaiian, Honolulu means "sheltered bay."

Cook Inlet: A 200-mile-long body of water extending from the Gulf of Alaska south of Homer all the way north past Anchorage to the Susitna (soo-SEAT-nah) Flats. The inlet was named for Captain James Cook, who explored the waters in 1778.

Knik Arm (KAH-nick arm): An Alaskan body of water forming the northernmost arm of Cook Inlet. Knik Arm connects Anchorage to the Matanuska (matt-ah-NOOSE-kah) Valley.

CHAPTER 2

Williwaw (willy-whaw): Strongest of Alaska's three most notorious winds. Williwaw's strong gusts can reach 115 miles per hour. The Chinook (SH-nook) is a warm winter wind that will melt ice or blow over power lines. Chinook is also another name for an Alaskan king salmon. Taku (tah-koo) is another gusting Alaskan wind with speeds to more than 100 miles per hour. The name comes from a glacier in southeast Alaska.

Malamute (mal-uh-myoot): The Alaskan malamute is a strong work dog weighing up to 115 pounds and bred to pull heavy sleds over long distances. Distinguishing features are a dark mask on the face or a cap over the head with a contrasting solid face color, with white fur on the underbody and some areas of the legs and feet. The malamute always has dark eyes, but the smaller Siberian husky has blue or brown eyes (sometimes one of each).

Wolverine (wool-ver-een): Largest of the weasel family measuring up to three and half feet long, this solitary carnivore is stocky and strong. It has a bad disposition and emits a terrible odor. A resident of far north forests, the wolverine has a light-brown stripe on each side of its shaggy, blackish fur.

Lower Forty-Eight: Always capitalized, this is the common Alaskan term for the continental United States (which excludes Hawaii).

Coastal brown: The largest of Alaska's bears, also called Kodiak or grizzly, it can weigh up to 1,500 pounds and reach 10 feet in height when standing on its hind legs. This dish-faced bear has a shoulder hump. It differs slightly from the Alaskan grizzly, which has blonde guard hairs and usually lives in the interior instead of along the coast. The classification as *Ursus horribilus* gives an indication of how it's regarded.

Banty (BAN-tee) *rooster*: Correctly called bantam and named after small domestic chickens that closely resemble standard breeds. The word is also used to describe a person of small stature, often with a combative nature.

Skookum (SKOO-kuhm): An Alaskan native word of high approval. It can mean brave, strong, or smart, depending on how it's used.

CHAPTER 3

Greenbelt: A narrow strip of land containing trees or other usually green plants, such as a park or farming land around a community.

Chugach (CHEW-gatch) *State Park*: A state-operated wilderness of 495,000 acres close to urban areas. The park is home to such birds as bald eagles, fish such as spawning salmon, and animals, including porcupine, lynx, wolf, black and brown bears, moose, beaver, and wolverine.

Moose rack: The antlers of a male or bull moose. In Alaska, laws require that the rack be at least 50 inches wide before the game animal may be shot.

CHAPTER 4

Birch (burr-ch): A usually small, short-lived deciduous tree having layered bark that easily peels off.

Chaise longue (shayz long): Commonly mispronounced as chaise lounge, this is a long reclining chair often used on decks, outdoors patios, and so on.

Plumeria (ploo-MAR-ee-yah): Also called frangipani

(FRAN-gee-PAN-ee). A shrub or small tree in Hawaii that produces large, fragrant blossoms. They are popular in leis, which are commonly worn around the neck.

Hibiscus (hi-BIS-cus): A common Hawaiian plant having a large, open blossom. Grown in a variety of colors, hibiscus is the state flower.

Bougainvillea (boo-gun-VEEL-ee-yah): A common tropical ornamental climbing vine in Hawaii with small flowers of many colors, including red, lavender, coral, and white.

Cow parsnips: A distinctive plant that grows up to 8 feet tall and blooms from July to mid-August in Alaskan woodlands or moist fields. The flower head size is so large that the plant is easily recognized. Some people are allergic to the leaves and stems.

Solstice (sole-stis): Either of the two times of the year when the sun is at the greatest distance from the equator. The summer solstice occurs around June 21/22 to begin summer in the northern hemisphere. The winter solstice happens around December 22 to begin winter in that same hemisphere.

CHAPTER 6

Bush: Always capitalized in Alaska, the term refers to the countless small, remote villages in the state's vast wilderness. Some villages are accessible only by plane, dogsled, or snowmobiles (which are called snow machines in Alaska).

Bush pilot: A daring pilot who flies a small airplane into remote areas. In Alaska, bush pilots land on almost any flat surface: gravel bars, beaches, glaciers, narrow rivers, and small clearings. It is said that a bush pilot considers it a good landing if he can walk away from where his aircraft touched down.

Floatplanes: Common in Alaska, this is a light aircraft with buoyant landing gear that allows taxiing for takeoff and landing on water.

Portuguese man-of-war: A common jellyfishlike creature in tropical seas with long, thin tentacles that can deliver severe stings to a swimmer.

Moray (MORE-ray) *eels*: A snakelike, sharp-toothed creature common in tropical seas. Eels are capable of inflicting severe bites to unwary swimmers or divers who put their hands or feet too near a hole in the lava where eels live.

Sea urchin: An undersea animal with a thin shell that's covered with sharp, movable spines. These can cause severe pain if stepped on.

CHAPTER 7

Hypothermia (hi-poe-THERM-ee-ah): A life-threatening condition that can lead to death when the body's inner or core temperature drops below 95 degrees Fahrenheit.

Seismograph (SIZE-moe-graf): An instrument that measures

and records ground vibrations of an earthquake.

CHAPTER 8

Mount McKinley (mac-KIN-lee): The tallest mountain in the United States towers 20,320 feet above sea level (over four miles). Located in central Alaska, the mountain was named after the twenty-fifth U.S. president, William McKinley. Most Alaskans prefer the name Denali. "The Mountain" (as it is commonly called by Alaska locals) is a popular tourist attraction, but few see it because it is usually hidden in clouds or rain.

Denali (duh-NAH-lee) *National Park*: An Alaskan Athabaskan (ath-ah-BAS-can) Indian word meaning "the great one." Denali refers both to Mount McKinley and the nearly six-million-acre national park that surrounds the mountain. A state park of nearly half a million acres is adjacent to the national park.

CHAPTER 9

Sow: The grown female of certain animals, including bears and hogs.

CHAPTER 10

Kayak (KY-yack): Originating with the Eskimos, this is the term for a small boat with a thin cover on a light framework. A flexible closure around the occupant's waist keeps the craft watertight.

Rainbow trout: A strong native fish related to the Pacific salmon and considered the hardest-fighting small-game fish. A colorful creature, it is usually greenish on top with a white belly. A pinkish stripe runs along both sides of the body. Many black dots are sprinkled over the fish's entire length.

Arctic char: A sea-run trout with light-colored spots. Some Alaskans say char is another name for a Dolly Varden trout. Commonly called a Dolly, the fish is named after a colorfully dressed character in one of Charles Dickens's novels. Char tend to weigh less than rainbow trout and are not considered to be the good fighters that rainbows are.

Chickadees (chik-ah-deez): Members of the American tit-mice family, these small birds are easily recognized by their repetitious and nasal call of *chick-a-dee-dee-dee*.

Juncos (junk-oes): Small birds of the American finch family, which are widely distributed in the United States and Canada.

White socks: An Alaskan black fly with white feet that is said to bite so savagely that it "seems to chew a hole in you." Some victims get a reaction to the welts left by the insect.

No-see-ums: A nearly invisible, black-and-white banded flying insect the size of a pinhead that can slip through small-mesh mosquito netting to annoy or bite people.

CHAPTER 11
God's eye is on the sparrow: The reference is to Luke 12:6-7.

"Are not five sparrows sold for two pennies? Yet not one of them is forgotten by God. Indeed, the very hairs of your head are all numbered. Don't be afraid; you are worth more than many sparrows" (NIV).

Boar: The grown male of certain animals, including bears and hogs.

Merganser (mehr-GAN-sir): Sometimes called a fish-eating duck in Alaska, these water fowl have a beak hooked at the end to help them feed on smolt (young salmon or sea trout). Mergansers usually have crested heads.